SPEAR

ALSO BY NICOLA GRIFFITH

So Lucky

Hild

Ammonite

Slow River

AUD TORVINGEN

The Blue Place

Stay

Always

NONFICTION

And Now We Are Going to Have a Party:
Liner Notes to a Writer's Early Life

SpEAR

NICOLA GRIFFITH

A TOM DOHERTY ASSOCIATES BOOK

NEW YORK

This is a work of fiction. All of the characters, organizations,
and events portrayed in this novel are either products of
the author's imagination or are used fictitiously.

SPEAR

Edited by Lydia Zoells

A Tordotcom Book
Published by Tom Doherty Associates
120 Broadway
New York, NY 10271

www.tor.com

Tor® is a registered trademark of Macmillan Publishing Group, LLC.

The Library of Congress Cataloging-in-Publication Data

Names: Griffith, Nicola, author.
Title: Spear / Nicola Griffith.
Description: First edition. | New York : Tordotcom, 2022. |
"A Tom Doherty Associates book."
Identifiers: LCCN 2021041760 (print) | LCCN 2021041761 (ebook) |
ISBN 9781250819321 (hardcover) | ISBN 9781250819338 (ebook)
Subjects: LCGFT: Novels.
Classification: LCC PS3557.R48935 S64 2022 (print) |
LCC PS3557.R48935 (ebook) | DDC 813/.54—dc23
LC record available at https://lccn.loc.gov/2021041760
LC ebook record available at https://lccn.loc.gov/2021041761

Our books may be purchased in bulk for promotional,
educational, or business use. Please contact your local bookseller or
the Macmillan Corporate and Premium Sales Department
at 1-800-221-7945, extension 5442, or by email at
MacmillanSpecialMarkets@macmillan.com.

First Edition: 2022

Printed in the United States of America

0 9 8 7 6 5 4 3 2

For Kelley, my love and my lake

SPEAR

IN the wild waste, a girl, growing. A girl at home in the wild, in the leafless thicket of thin grey saplings with moss growing green on one side. In this thicket, the moss side does not face north but curves in a circle with its back to the world, and, at its centre, where the branches grow most tangled and forbidding, is a hill. In the face of that hill, always hidden from the world, is the dark mouth of the cave where the girl lives with her mother.

As far as the girl can tell, none on two legs but herself and her mother has ever trod here. Her mother will creep from the cave only as far as the gardens at the edge of the thicket, and then only in summer when the leaves are cloak enough to hide the sun-burnished bronze of her heavy-waved hair, when the hard enamel blue of her eyes might be forget-me-nots; but the girl is at home in all the wild. She roams the whole of Ystrad Tywi, the valley of the Tywi who fled Dyfed in the Long Ago. In this valley, where there is a tree she will climb it; it will shelter her, and the birds that nest there in spring will sing to her, warning of any two-legged approach. In May, as the tree blossoms fall and herbs in the understorey flower, she will know by the scent of each how it might taste with what meat, whether it might heal, who it could kill. From its nectar she will know which moths will come to drink, know too of the bats that catch the moths, and what nooks they return to where they hang wrapped in their leather shrouds as the summer sun climbs high, high enough to shine even into the centre of the thicket. Before harvest, when the bee hum spreads drowsy and heavy as honey, she tastes in their busy drone a tale of the stream over which they skim, the falls down which the stream pours, the banks it winds past where reeds grow thick and the autumn bittern booms. And when the snow begins to fall once again, she catches a flake on her tongue and feels, lapping against her belly, the lake it was drawn from by summer sun, far away—a lake like a promise she will one day know. Then as the world folds down for winter, so too do the girl and her mother, listening to the crackle of flame and, beyond the leather door curtain, the soft hiss of snow settling over the hills and hollows like white felt.

IN THE CAVE is a great hanging bowl. "My cup," her mother calls it, when she tells her stories. On warm days, bright precious days when her mother will venture outside under the sun—beckon a bird to her finger and sing with it its song—the cup is a gift to the laughing, blue-eyed Elen from her lover, the girl's father with grey-green eyes like the sea. On these days, her mother calls the girl Dawnged: her blessing, her gift and favour. The girl likes this name, and these days when the bowl is just a bowl, and they work together in the garden while her mother tells tales of the Tuath Dé, the sidhe gods who came to Eiru-over-the sea with four great treasures, one each from the four islands of the Overland that drowned. The Tuath are forever squabbling over the treasures.

"There is the Dagda, with his midnight steed. His treasure was the greatest of all, the golden cup—No, not so deep with the beans, Dawnged." And the girl would push the next bean less far down into its long, heaped line of dirt. "Now, this cup— Do you remember the cup, little gift?"

And the girl would say, "Yes!" and tell of how the Morrigan, whose steed was grey, had stolen it from the Dagda for herself, and how her lover, Manandán, son of the sea and raiser of mists, had stolen it from her in turn. And she would ask, "What else is the Morrigan called?" Or, "What other name has the Dagda?" But her mother would just hug her, tell her never to steal, for stealing wore away one's soul, then laugh and ruffle her hair and kiss her eyes—"So like them both"—and they would promise each other they would stay together in the cave, always.

On these fine days when her mother was herself, the girl heard tales, too, of Lugh of the shining spear, and Elatha, keeper of the stone. She heard of Núada the king, who held the sword of light—until Bres, Elatha's son, took it, and Núada must be content with a silver arm. And Bres, Núada, and Lugh each had only one name.

But the stories changed with the weather. On dark autumn days, when the wind moaned and stripped the last forlorn leaves from the trees, when it fretted and worried

3

at their peace, thrusting its tongue deep into their warm cave—trying to lick them out as the girl had seen a badger lick out ants from a tree—on those days her mother grew gaunt and strange. The child would wake in the night to her mother's dream cries—a man coming to steal her, steal her child, steal her payment—and her mother would not eat, only hunch over the bowl and scry, and follow the girl about with haunted eyes. She would shout at the girl and rant, confusing her, confusing the tales, for now Elen herself was in them. In these tales the cup was not a gift; it was thrice-stolen, it was payment. In these tales Manandán was a cruel trickster who came with his cup to Dyfed, following the raiding men of Eiru, and found Elen, Elen whose magics were fragile and human against the might of the Tuath Dé, and there he took her by force and kept her prisoner, his willing—no, not willing, compelled to be willing—slave, until the day she fled, taking the golden cup as payment. She fled, and hid herself inside the cave of stolen trophies: the cup she stole from its first thief; herself who was stolen, and stole herself back; and the gift she stole that he knows nothing of.

On these days, Elen calls the girl Tâl, her payment. "Because I am owed, Tâl, I am owed. He owes me, yes, for possessing my soul and my mind; and the other owes me, too, because he knew. Oh, he knew what Manandán would do. But they will never find us, no. We will stay hidden, we will stay safe, and they will never know your true name."

She will never say what the girl's true name is, or who the other was, and the stories are never the same. And always the cave is hidden.

THE BOWL IS not gold, it is not silver, nor even beaten bronze; it is enamel on black iron that never dulls and never dents, though sometimes the iron shimmers with light reflected from elsewhere. Even direct from the hearth it will not burn the hand that holds it, and any who drink from it are healed. Or so Elen tells the girl. The girl herself cannot tell because she drinks and eats from the bowl every day, but every day she grows tall and taller, strong and stronger; her hair with the same heavy wave as her mother's but paler, brass where her mother's is bronze, her eyes sea grey with a hint of green. With her fingers she traces the bowl's wondrous twining beasts of inlaid bronze, their raised wings and bright glass eyes; she touches the cold, enamelled escutcheons where great hooks hold the bowl when it hangs, and pushes with her palm the four small iron stumps on the base on which it stands by the hearth; she smooths the sharp etched points of the mounted knights' spears, the clean lines of the swords they wield in endless battle.

The girl grows fleet. She runs with the deer. She learns to hunt with Cath Linx of the tufted ears, bathing in the joy of the stalk and the savage leap. She hunts, too, with traps, with sling and stone, and with her one knife, honed to a bright shard; she no longer weeps when she takes the fawn or the hare, for she and her mother must eat; though, more than once, she has left the leveret in its scrape, and wished the sloe-eyed hare the best for her young. As she grows and her legs stretch, she roams farther; she ranges a mile, a league, three leagues, ten. It is wild land, long abandoned to the wet and the cold and, since the Redcrests left, claimed by no king, though once it was, and one day would be again. She climbs an elm whose new leaves taste like sorrel, an elm with no name but Elm. Sometimes Elm rocks her gently to sleep in the late spring breeze, or whispers to her of how it is to grow from a sapling, to draw water from deep in the earth, to feel the world turn season after season, and once Elm shows her the sparrowhawk that waits with marigold eyes for the mistle thrush to leave the safety of its nest. She follows a rivulet to a small, hidden pond where a duck has laid her eggs, and this pond she keeps hidden from the foxes and from Cath Linx, and visits sometimes to delight with the ducklings as they splash for the first time, shake their wings out, get lost and are called back safe to their mother, the duck that has no name but Duck.

And when she, too, goes back to her mother, cheeks blooming fresh with wild roaming, her mother weeps and begs her to stay close, stay safe—for the girl is hers, her gift, her treasure, her payment, all she has—but the girl feels her growing strength; she must run, she must climb, she must test her power.

On one far roam she follows a twining wisp of blue-grey smoke south, down the valley where it begins to widen, and comes to a new steading, built by the ruin of one abandoned in the Long Ago to the wet and the cold. But the land now is drying and warming, and folk are creeping back: real people, not from stories. Hidden in a copse of hazel, she watches and listens as the folk move about the new-built roundhouse with the blue smoke seeping from the pointed roof. They speak a language like hers, but not quite: blunter and rough-hewn, blurred by time. They have names, each different, one that is theirs alone. A name, she thinks, is what makes a person who they are. A name is how they know themself.

These folk are not like her and not like her mother; some are differently shaped, their voices rough and deep as a low-ing cow. She stalks two as they walk beyond their thorn hedge to a stand of alders by the stream near their house. They are noisy; their untidy feet snap twigs and kick stones without heed for what might hear. They talk but the things they speak of—fleece and shearing and wives—mean noth-ing to her. One is bigger than the other, older, but both have reddish gold hair on their faces, wispy as a billy goat's beard. Their skin is like tanned leather and they do not smell like her and her mother—who in winter smell of woodsmoke and deep furs, grease and ash, and in summer of the herbs they crush in the pool to bathe, and the pale yellow wine they make in the month of honey. These people smell of sweat and iron and sheepskin.

She crouches in the damp, loamy undergrowth and watches as they cut the alders down to stumps, and pile the wood into heaps. She does not watch the wood or the bend and flex of their legs as they swing; she watches the tools: the small, sharp hatchet and the long axe. After the wood is piled, the two sit awhile; she waits patiently. When they sigh and haul themselves to their feet she follows them back to the thorn hedge enclosing their house, watches them walk through the gap that is their gate and fasten a thorn hurdle across the gap. She climbs a hazel tree in the copse and sees one hang his axe from a nail by the doorjamb and the other chunk his hatchet into the stump by the door. They go in.

The house is secure against the drawing dark. Or so they think. In the hazel copse she waits silent as stone for the drop of dark's curtain. When it falls she steals past their thorn hedge and pulls the hatchet from the stump, tucks it in her belt, and lifts the axe onto her shoulder. It is hafted with good elm, smooth already from a year's use. She touches the cold iron. A good blade. An hour later she returns and from the nail hangs a brace of hare, and on the stump leaves a comb of honey.

In the months that follow, word spreads among the new-made steadings: the fey are abroad, invisible, of course, as told in the stories, but also nothing like the stories, for they seek bright iron. She listens to them, unseen, and smiles to herself as they whisper that no man may leave an awl or a chisel for a moment unwatched, or it will vanish; no woman may leave her basket untended, or the yarn, with its needles and shears, will melt into the air like mist in the sun. And sometimes they leave out a hunk of cheese or a cake of barley bread, and speak aloud a favour, and she will find their lost goat, or pull up the stubborn stump from their field before dawn. Meanwhile, in the cave, the stick furniture that had been good enough for a small, desperate woman and her infant is replaced by sturdy chairs and a table of felled timber, split and dressed. They no longer sleep on the floor by the hearth but on a fine frame with a woven leather platform. And the girl has listened so often to the speech of those who never saw her that sometimes their rough-hewn words creep into her mouth, and her mother flinches at the sound of the outside world. At these times she begs the girl again, begs Dawnged, her blessing, her gift, to turn her back on the world beyond. And the girl says, "But that world is full of people who belong to their place, who belong to one another, who belong to themselves. And they have names! Out in the world all is different and new!"

⌘

SO IT WAS that her mother, to keep the girl interested, taught her the language of books, and with great reluctance showed the girl her chest of scrolls. "These are tales of the world," she told her. "All the adventure, all the different and new you need." The tales of heroes and great deeds, and the riddles and tragic tales, did interest the girl, but many were stories of how to bind a wound and grow a garden, how to husband a flock and dress a fresh-killed fowl, and she already knew these things. And all the people in the stories had names, and she did not; and she would never find her name here in the cave.

She began to roam again. Now that she knew what the marks meant, she saw stones carved with them, names that she spoke aloud to herself. *Of the daughter of Cunignos, Avittoriga* or *Put here by the hand of Maglicunos, man of Elmet.* And from these she learnt another language, one not taught by her mother: the language of scratches cut along the edges of the marker stones, deep cuts that one by one she matched to the letter of the words of the book language carved on the

9

stones' faces. A side and secret tongue cut not by the men of Dyfed but by those from Eiru-over-the-sea. She ran her fingertips over the lichened stone. When a time came to carve her name, would it be *Dawnged, girl of Ystrad Tywi* or *Tâl, payment to Elen,* or would she one day find her true name?

One winter—so harsh she rarely ventured far, for her footprints in the deep snow would lead any with eyes to their cave—wolves howled around about and she saw strange men on the old tracks. Ragged men, grim men with weeping wounds and missing teeth, sometimes with women, hard and thin as whips. She followed them, stepping high in and out of the deep snow, silent as a doe, and listened. Often these folk did not use names. Often they savaged the folk of a steading, and burnt and stole, and sometimes they would kill one another over a crust of bread, and sometimes wolves would kill one, or two, and sometimes two or three would kill a wolf. She saw more blood in the snow that winter than she had in the whole of her life.

That winter, too, she saw blood in her own drawers—not sharp-tanged like fresh blood, but strangely sweet—and in spring the world began to smell different. The urge to roam increased upon her like thirst.

Now when she spied on women and men she crept close and closer, closer than was safe, because she was drawn to the curve of a hip, the gleam of sweat on a throat, and she longed to feel the weight of glossy hair on her skin. For one pretty young wife she found a perfect stone and left it for her to find, and when the girl returned and found it gone, she plucked and left a sweet-smelling violet, then hid herself to watch. When the young wife saw the flower, she turned it in her hand, smiled a private smile, and with lips like plums blew a kiss towards the wood. The girl dreamt of the woman for a month.

The summer passed like a wide blue dream; she slept little, but roamed hill and valley, wood and mountainside. One midday she gazed at herself in the ducklings' pool— ducklings long flown now—where the water lay still by the rushes, gazed at her brass hair and eyes the cool, green-tinted grey of the sea. *Who am I?* She looked nothing like that young wife, and nothing like the men with hair on their faces. Her mother's hair, almost, but not her eyes. She touched the pool and felt the echo of that faraway lake, the promise of all that was wide and bright and clear that she would one day find. But not this day. This day she was charged by a ram.

She was up the hillside where the sheep of the first stead- ing were hefted, seeing but not seeing the ewes with well- grown lambs, because she was full of the remembered song of the lake, when a fly hurrying by brushed her arm and she knew in an instant that it was flown from the dirt caked around the legs of a ram—the ram charging her for com- ing too close to his ewes. Most days she would have run, would have leapt away and laughed and scolded the ram till he stopped, but today she was full of her own strength and dreams, and today she turned, took the ram by his horns, and forced him to his knees. And when he charged again, this time she took him by the horns and threw him to one side. Stood over him as he lay there, stunned, and said, "I have bested you in battle!" And she had, a battle as fierce as any fought by knight and dragon.

That autumn, her mother was wild with grief and ragged with rage; she would not eat; she would not speak to the girl but to shout her name Tâl as a curse, a warning. "He is looking for me, he is looking!" The girl soothed her as best she could and lay awake buffeted in her body by the same winds as the skeins of geese flowing in the river of air above. The autumn echoed and ran with wild magic; her fate was near, she felt it in her blood and bone and heartbeat, in the whirl of wet brown leaves and wingbeat overhead.

Winter was harsher than the one before, and from the birds and badgers and foxes and stoats she heard rumour of a great new band of bandits. Grim and fierce, said the badger; sharp-eyed and cunning, said the fox. She remembered the ram. She could best them in battle; she could! And she longed to escape the cave and her mother and find adventure. Find her true self.

One morning she woke to find the bright, glittering cold changed to dull grey and the drip, drip of icicles thawing. She knew from the sleeping grumble of a hedgepig turning in her den that it would be a brief thaw, but for now her footsteps might blend into the melt and be hidden. She took up her axe and went looking for battle.

She loped over the hills, then south down the valley, scenting the air, asking the worms deep in the dirt: *Where are they?* She found nothing until on the eastern slope of the valley, farther south than she had been before, she trod on

snow which did not give like snow, and her stride stuttered, and she stumbled. She dug in the snow and found an arm, with black hair curling from beneath its cuff. She dug more and uncovered a man, long dead, much eaten by beasts. She squatted in the snow and laid a hand on the shattered thigh bone of his left leg and caught a small, mournful memory of falling from the saddle; a prayer in some smoky, spiky tongue that almost made sense; and blood pooling on the turf, turf that was brown with the end of summer. She sought for more, but, faint to begin with, the memory blew away in the wind. She brought her attention back to the body before her. Over a glittering shirt—sewn with shiny overlapping metal, like fish scales—he wore a wide leather belt hung crosswise, and from it hung a blade in a scabbard.

She saw that the scabbard could be unhooked, lifted it off, and drew the blade with some difficulty: it was rusted in places, and the tip was missing, but it was a sword, like the swords of the knights who chased the dragons around the bowl. She swang it with one hand, then the other; it was not very big. She resheathed it and laid it to one side. On a smaller belt around his hips was a fine bright purse and a good knife with silver-inlaid hilt. On his left hand, a ring with a reddish stone carved with a strange beast, perhaps a fish, only balanced upright on its tail. She dug further, and found a spear, two spears as she had seen the knights carry tied to the saddle of their horses. But there was no horse and no shield, no pack of food or bedroll or travelling cloak that she could see. She piled her spoils, said a blessing, as she would to a dead hare, then left him exposed so that hungry beasts might find his bones and feed their young.

Just inside the thicket, hidden from the world and also from her mother, she laid out her finds in the weak waterlight of winter. The purse was bright but empty except for a worn silver coin with a Redcrest king's head—emperor, in the language of the scrolls. The small belt was no better than her own, so she set it aside for use on the coop she meant to build for the ducklings she would catch for her mother when the duck eggs hatched. The fish-scale shirt was made of thin, supple leather, with each scale sewn on with sinew. When she tried it, it was tight at the shoulder, tighter across the chest, and too short for her arms. Did its magic work? It had not saved the man who wore it. Perhaps there was no magic for falling off your own mount and dying alone and unmarked. Perhaps its magic was only against blades. There was a tear in the leather on the right side, repaired and cleverly hidden by the scales. The spears were good straight ash. One thick-shafted, with a broad leaf-shaped blade and two wide flanges beneath that, the other a slimmer shaft topped not with a blade but a long point, as thick as her middle finger with hammer marks plain on the tapering sides, and sharp-tipped, even now. Different heads for different uses, though she did not yet know what. The knife had a good blade but she preferred her own. The baldric was sturdy leather, stiff now from lying in the snow, but sound. And last, the sword. The scabbard was wool-lined wood wrapped in carved leather with a heavy tip of silver. The tip was etched with what might be faint figures, blurred and worn with age, and the leather had once been green, or perhaps blue like that wrapped around the hilt, and wound about with black wire: a strange, rough leather, with stipples. The pommel had once held a stone but now gaped empty. She drew the blade and shook the scabbard to see if the missing blade tip might fall out; none did. The wire-and-leather grip felt good in her hand, sure and light. But she did not swing the sword. She laid it on the fish-scale shirt and studied it carefully. The metal rippled and flowed where it was not rusted. This was a fine thing, wounded but not dead, and if she worked steadily she could bring it back to health by spring.

THAT LAST MONTH of winter, as she laboured over the sword and its scabbard, her mother would cajole her, beg her Dawnged to stop, and when the girl did not, Elen became silent, her eyes dark at the centre, dark as ink dropped in blue dye, and ringed with charcoal. Elen grew frantic as the girl worked; she wept and muttered, and cried out in her sleep for Tâl, but the girl kept working, scouring off the rust, honing the blade, greasing the metal with the last of their duck fat, relining the scabbard with sheepskin stolen from a farm, replacing the little leather ties and their broken enamelled cairns at the ends with copper blobs she learnt to melt in her homemade crucible. She knew her mother scryed and wove spells when she left with her spears and learnt how to hurl them, but she did not care. She threw and threw until both spears always struck their target; she learnt that the broad-headed one would not fall out of a running deer but would drag it to a halt, and the other one could punch through metal—had punched through the arm of the fish-scale shirt. A hunting spear, and a spear for hunting men, armed men: a battle spear. She did not know how to mend the fish scale, which she had split, so she cut the leather shirt down the back to make it wider, to fit, took out the broken scales, and sewed in their place, and down the new leather in the back, small oblongs of wood wrapped in boiled leather and dyed dark with oak gall. The leather baldric she soaked in fat rendered from a wild pig, and soaked again, until it was as supple as a length of cloth.

One afternoon when winter was done and the world had begun its turn towards the light, with green shoots thrusting through the dark earth, the girl roamed the high fell in the steeper, northern part of the valley. And even here men were coming again with their sheep; she found droppings and followed them—followed the complaint from an old wether with worn teeth that this time perhaps the woman who herded them would leave them their wool until it was warmer. She was smiling to herself about the foolish old sheep, and sending it news of where it might find tender grass suitable for its mouth, when she heard a savage snarl, and ran. She leapt a tangle of gorse, and found a stray ewe with one lamb at her tail backing away from a wild dog that looked to be half wolf, standing over one already-dead lamb, hackles raised, and thinking, *Kill them all, kill kill kill*. She threw her hunting spear and took the dog through the side of its chest, tearing its heart. "Hush," she told the ewe and her living lamb, promised she would use the dead lamb with all reverence, and showed them the way back to the flock.

When they were upwind, she gralloched the lamb, drained it, and buried the guts so as not to draw more predators to the sheep. She slung the carcass on her shoulder—it was a good one, fat with new grass, and would feed her and her mother for a week; the shepherd could spare one lamb, for she could have lost two—and turned for home. But as she reached the lower trackway, she heard something new: jingling. Jingling and hooves. She stilled, unmoving as a stump, and blended into the mix of evergreen, bare twig, and white-blossomed hawthorn that ran alongside the track. A company of men, a score or more, cantered by. They wore mail shirts—some ringed, some sewn plates, some fish scale—and helmets, and swords, and shields with painted devices, and their mounts glittered with gold at tailpiece, headpiece, and saddle. Two carried spears like standards, with little bannerlets fluttering from the top. One, his helm tucked under his arm against the blue-and-brown leather of his tunic, had gleaming dark skin, almost as dark as the bowl, with the hair on his head springy and tight-curled as a sheep's and none on his chin; another was milk-pale and speckled as a thrush's breast; a third, lean and lithe in plain black, above which his face and neck showed the rich brown of walnut; and another had sloping shoulders and a belly rounded as a duck egg—and his skin eggshell smooth. All different yet somehow alike—not family but easy with one another, and loud, laughing and singing, bright and clean.

The same bright, the same clean she remembered from the scent of the promised lake. The girl's heart soared: a story come alive from legend, knights hunting dragons!

When they were safely past she draped her lamb over a boundary stone, wrote with a piece of chalk on the side of the stone *Mine, touch not!* in the language of books, and again in the straight scratch-marks of the language of Eiru, and ran after the knights.

They were moving fast on tall horses; she did not have them in sight when they found their quarry. Or, rather, when their quarry found them: not dragons but bandits. They were ambushed by well-organised fighters—there were more bandits than knights, many more, and more vicious. There was no glorious charge as in the stories, only men running under horses' bellies and slashing them open, rusty knives sneaking into gaps in armour, the shock of bright banners falling, and then the knights—strong and fresh and well fed—tightening their reins and drawing their swords. And it seemed to the girl as she ran towards them with the speed of a loping wolf that if their horses had not responded so fast many more knights would have fallen in that first rush—and more even than that, for now the girl was among them, unseen, saving many with a quick, hidden thrust from a hedge, a fast slash from behind a tree, and a lithe dance alongside a riderless horse—who understood her gestured request and sheltered her from sight—to hamstring a bandit looming over a dazed, bare-headed knight. The knight—the milk-faced one, in brave green-and-yellow leathers—had lost his helm and taken a blow from a stave alongside his temple. She saved him, unseen—though perhaps he did see her, for his eyes widened before she whirled away. But she had seen the weight of the blow he took; he might survive but likely would not remember.

Then the knights settled into their grim killing, for once over their shock they were skilled and fast, and the girl watched the flickering sword work of the man in black leather who stayed on his horse, the brave charge of the one in blue-and-brown leathers—though in a helmet now—who cast a spear then leapt from his horse and fought back-to-back with another with a lush, curling beard until no bandits were left. And after, when they were gathering themselves up and collecting their riderless horses—which the girl had persuaded to stand quietly outside the fighting until called for—she scooped up a fallen leather cap with cheek flaps, for she had seen what could happen to a bare head.

She watched them get their breath, strip the bandits—one exclaimed at a shield he found—bind their own wounds, bind their horses' wounds, and take stock before riding slowly back down the valley, two bodies slung over horses' backs, and many men walking to save their own wounded mounts. She shadowed them as they walked—the man in black limped, though she could tell it was an old limp, and familiar, as much a part of him as breathing—ghosting along, listening, drawing even closer when they stopped at dusk and built a fire, dulling their night sight.

They spoke more like her mother than the folk of the fell, though the limping man in black spoke with a rise and fall that spoke to her of mountains in another land, and the lush-bearded man with an accent scented with sun-warmed fruit and wine. The dazed man in green and yellow seemed high in their company but allowed himself to be told what to do, which was to sit down and keep still, because he had staggered when he dismounted, and staggered again when he tried to fill a pot with water. His ears must have been ring-ing, or perhaps he was angry, because he shouted rather than spoke.

His beardless friend in brown-and-blue leathers looked up from the shield he was examining and said, "Oh, just admit it, Cei. Your horse threw you; he likes you as little as you like him."

She listened to the horses, found Cei's bay gelding: it was true, there was no love between the two; Cei was . . . afraid of his horse? No, not afraid, exactly. The bay showed her the way he sat: tight, hunched, fretful of falling and being humiliated.

Cei said, "I was pushed. By some beardless stripling who then for some unaccountable reason used a boar spear like an axe—a boar spear! He swung at me with such force that when he missed he took off the leg of one of his fellow peas-ants. Which poured blood like a river and ruined my tunic."

The man in black looked up. "A stripling you say? Took off a man's leg with a boar spear?"

"Fearsome," said the one in brown and blue.

Cei plucked at his red-stained tunic and frowned. "Just big and stupid. My head hurts. Is there wine, Lance?"

Lance, the man in black, shook his head and gestured at the man in brown and blue. "Bedwyr drank it all."

Bedwyr, who had opened his mouth to deny it, saw Lance's slight head shake, and lifted the shield instead. "Perhaps it was your fearsome peasant who took Talorcan." He traced something on the shield, and sighed.

In the flickering flame light, the girl saw painted on the shield the same strange upright fish beast carved into the ring she had found on the dead man. His device. *Talorcan*. Even the dead had names. But the man named Talorcan, or who at least had worn Talorcan's ring, died alone, and died before the bandit band came to the valley. The bandits must have found his horse, or perhaps what the wolves had left of his horse, and the shield still tied behind the saddle.

The men ate, and talked of Talorcan, who had left on a quest nearly a year ago. They addressed many of their remarks to Cei; they were keeping him awake, she thought.

On the other side of the fire, closer to her, the one with the curled beard looked up from cleaning his sword and said, in his sunlit accent, to Bedwyr, "They weren't all peasants."

"No?" Bedwyr said. Then to Lance, "Andros thinks we weren't fighting peasants."

Lance limped over to join them. "No. Some were fighting men. We have faced them before, I think, and taken their surrender."

Andros went back to his sword, and Bedwyr said softly to Lance, "Did you see this fearsome stripling among the dead?"

"No," said Lance just as softly. "And I wonder if he was our helper."

"Helper?"

Lance nodded. "Did you not feel it?"

"No," Bedwyr said, but he fingered something that glinted silver, hanging like an amulet around his neck.

"I thought I saw from the corner of my eye something moving, just after you cast your javelin."

"Something?"

"It moved lithe as a cat."

"A cat? You dreamed it."

"Did I dream all the dead? We had help; it was too easy."

"Easy?" said Bedwyr. "We lost two Companions and three mounts—to what should have been a rabble of bandits. Who knew there could be so many in this forsaken valley?"

To the girl it was clear Lance was thinking much he was not willing to say. In the end he said only, "We would have lost more without our mysterious helper who has melted away like mist."

"And will you tell that to the king?" Bedwyr dropped his amulet, a cross, beneath his tunic.

Lance rubbed his face and looked at Cei, who was now playing a lethargic game of knucklebones with the egg-shaped man. "I don't know. Perhaps I'll suggest we should not yet reclaim the Valley of the Tywi. The whole thing has the smell of the uncanny."

Bedwyr touched his chest where the cross hung out of sight. "That's business for Myrddyn."

Lance nodded. The girl could tell he did not like this man whose business was the uncanny. "Perhaps I'll know what to tell Artos king when we get back to Caer Leon."

Artos, she thought. *A king. In Caer Leon.* The words rang in her head like a bell, like the scent of the lake, like the bright clean shimmer around the Companions.

She withdrew to the shadows and began the long walk back under a thick twist of stars.

No one had touched her lamb—of course they had not, for they thought it belonged to the fey—so she gathered both spears in one hand and hoisted the lamb's loose weight back over her shoulder. The shafts of both spears—*a boar spear,* she thought; *a javelin*—were sticky with blood. She looked at her big hand, red now. Men's blood. She had killed a man; more than one man. The world looked no different, but she felt different in it, as though it had tilted on its axis and the line of stars had changed.

She cleaned herself and her spears before she found her way back to the thicket, and finding her way took more time than it should, almost as though she were a stranger and her mother's warding geas worked against her. As though she no longer belonged.

As though she could smell the change, her mother would not at first speak to her, and then began to shout wild accusations: Did the girl want them to be found? Did she want her mother's mind rived from her body and that body used like a rag? Did she want her mother to lose everything, every single thing she had earned? And after her rant she fell into moaning, and then into silence. It would pass, the girl knew. Meanwhile, she ate and slept, hunted and foraged, and her mother just followed the girl with her haunted forget-me-not blue eyes, drew figures in the hearth ash and cast bones, and jumped at strange noises.

After two days of this, the girl sat by her mother, took her mother's hand, and said, "What is my name?"

Elen's hand lay limp in the girl's.

"I need a name."

But Elen looked at nothing, or something only she could see.

❧

THE GIRL REMADE her shoes with thicker soles suitable for a long journey; she cut back her hair to fit under the leather cap, and slowly let herself understand why she was collecting or making or repurposing many things they already had—flint strike light, a second hatchet, whetstone and leather water bottle, needle and thread, wound herbs. So on the day she found herself binding her breasts and dropping the fish-scale shirt over her finest wool tunic, her heart tripped for a moment but she was surprised only by it being today that she could no longer wait. She nodded, and after a moment cinched her sturdy belt around her waist and from that hung her own knife—the other, Talorcan's, she would leave for her mother—and the bright purse. As the embers in the hearth began to dim, into that bright purse she put the worn silver coin and flint stone arrow point with the carved spiral she had found but not yet given to the young farm-wife, the carnelian ring, and her careful bundle of tinder, which left room for the whetstone, a coil of spare twine, half a lamb sausage, a twist of fruit leather, one withered apple, and a wrapped lump of grey bog butter dug from their cask. In her belt she tucked the hatchet. And then she hung the baldric over her shoulder, and from that the sword tied into its scabbard. She set her hand on the hilt and settled the unaccustomed weight.

The girl looked at the only home she had known, the furniture she had built with her own hands, the beautiful bowl by the hearth still as new as the day the smith made it, and at her mother, who sat as though made of stone facing the cooling hearth with her back to the entrance and to the girl.

"Mother?"

Her mother did not move and made no sound. And the girl saw for the first time that here and there the heavy bronze glinted with streaks of tin.

"I have need of a name."

Silence.

"I must go. But I'll keep safe, and I will be back."

She put on her cap.

"Mother?" She took off the cap so she might hear a reply. "Elen?"

Nothing but the sigh of embers into ash.

At the cave mouth the girl took the spears from where they leaned against the rock, and lifted the leather door curtain.

"He will find you," Elen said. "Beyond this cave and this valley he will scent you on the wind. And when he does he will come to claim what is his. I will never see you again. I loved you, child, loved you so much I did not name you, for naming calls. But now you are leaving, and I will give you

26

your name. The four treasures of the Tuath are the sword, which is given, the stone, which is hidden, the cup, which I have, and the spear. You are that spear. You are my Bêrhyddur, my spear enduring. You are Peretur. Know that I do not remove my ward, and under my geas will remain hidden, even from you. Know, too: you have broken my heart."

And the girl, Peretur, longed to run to her mother, throw her arms around her as she had as a child, and be folded into her warmth and woman smell and never have to face the outside world alone. But she did not, for then she would never leave. And now that she had her name, she understood that a name was only part of what she searched for. She must find the rest. "Fare well," she said. And stepped from the cave.

Outside in the clearing her feet faltered but she walked on, through the thicket, and once on the other side she felt in her heart a snapping, like the parting of a sinew.

❧

SHE HAD A horse now, a sorry-looking gelding with a bony face who had been badly treated by his former owner. He had come to the girl's hand willingly when she called, then patiently taught her how to ride, though he refused the bit.

After some months on the road she was taller still, her muscles hard but her smile more ready. With so much time in the sun her heavy brass hair gleamed with strands of gold. She found she liked the company of others, liked exchanging a week's work—as she travelled east the land grew flatter and richer, and shepherds became farmers, and there was always work—for ten days' food for herself and Bony, or five

days' work for new breeks in good green wool. She longed
for fine dyed leather, like the Companions of the king—
Arturus, whom only the Companions called Artos—but
such leather was expensive and only to be found in the company of kings. Those she met were wary at first—they saw
the horse and sword, they saw the fish-mail and spears and
heard the way she spoke, and hid their gold and their daugh-
ters. But she learnt to hide most of her strength, hide her real
self, drop her voice, and use the rougher tongue the common folk spoke on the fellside; she learnt to use her soft face,
hard muscles, and sweet smile to remind them of some son
or nephew or long-ago sweetheart. And then they saw the
careful mends of mismatched gear and the missing pommel
stone, the bony unbitted horse, and set aside their misgivings
for a while. Then she would tell them her name, or part
of her name—Per, a stripling making his way to Arturus
king's court at Caer Leon to offer his services—and they
would look at the old sword and shake their heads, and tell
him, not unkindly, to go home, go back to his ma and da and
not get mixed up the doings of high folk. She would smile
in her turn and simply repeat that she would find her way, if
they would only give her directions. And they did, and more
besides. One bold farmwife—*Call me Blodwen*—when her
husband was unhitching the oxen from the plough, took the
girl's hand, kissed her on the cheek, and whispered in her
ear that she reckoned she could help Peretur find his way
around quite handily, then placed the girl's hand on her soft
yielding breast, mouthed *Moonrise,* closed one bright brown
eye in a knowing wink, and went to see to her husband.

That night before moonrise Peretur sneaked to the byre, saddled Bony, and fled without her payment. As she rode, her dreams filled with that yielding breast and warm breath and those luscious lips until she thought she might run mad. For a while she steered herself only to jobs with men, until she found some men also might make hot eyes and promises. The thought of kissing one of them filled her with nothing but refusal, and she knew she would not play with a woman who might feel deceived, so for a while she learnt not to speak to others at all but keep to herself.

Always she travelled south and east, following the pull of all that was bright and clear, the song and promise of the lake. She cut her hair shorter, kept her mail shirt in her saddlebag and her cap and sword tied behind the cantle half hidden by her bedroll, though there was nothing she could do to hide the spears. But more folk now carried spears, and there were more strangers, and a mix of folk—and now not all skin was pale, not all hair was bright, and not all men's faces had hair. Folk became less wary. Soon she could stop at places thronged with people, a dozen, two dozen, so many she could turn aside interest deftly with a smile or a word, for she found speaking made folk less suspicious than not speaking. And in this way by the week before Harvest Day she found herself in a village three miles from Caer Leon.

◌◌◌

THE VILLAGE WAS full of people, more people than Peretur had seen in one place at one time, three score or more. She found her way to the village well, where she helped an old man with a crooked back to haul a bucket for himself and his ass. He thanked her, and she mentioned all the people.

"Aye," he said. "Harvest week. Crowds on top of crowds."

"Any work for me, d'ye suppose?"

"No doubt, no doubt, a strong lad like you. Try Modron at the inn, or Hywel at the byre. Though either way you'll need Modron's word. Good day to ye, lad." He and his ass moved into the street.

She filled another bucket for Bony and while he drank dipped out a cup for herself.

Thinking perhaps she should camp beyond the village, avoid all these people who filled her head with their concerns, she bent her head to the cup—and, with her first sip, into her mouth swam a fish, and another finned dreamily in the shadowed overhang of a lake bank, and her mind filled with a tall forest of underwater weeds through which an eel ribboned. She swallowed, and her heart filled with light, the light she had known as a child. It was here. Here.

She led Bony to the inn and byre, next to each other. The old man was right; it was crowded. And the street was so thronged he and his ass were not very far ahead of her.

She stopped a dull-looking youth in the street. "I'm looking for—"

Three children ran past, shrieking, startling the old man's ass, which kicked out and in turn upset the pony pulling an overloaded cart, and between one breath and the next people were shouting, the ass braying, and a horse shattering the air with a panicked scream.

She dropped Bony's reins, leapt for the ass and soothed it with a word, then hauled on the headstall of the pony telling it to *Stop, stop, was it a gangling foal to get so confused by a mere donkey?* It hung its head, shamefaced, and suffered itself to be led sweetly to the side so that people could come pick up the fallen sacks.

"Boy!" A thick-waisted woman was pointing to him. "You, yes you. I've work for you if you want it."

Peretur patted the pony once more; he seemed settled.

"I'm Modron," the woman said. "This is my byre and my inn. Come closer. What's your name?" When Peretur came close, and gave her name, Modron gave her a piercing look, then shrugged. "Peretur is it? Well, Peretur, go find Hywel and tell him—tell his boy—I said you're to sleep in the hay loft and eat with us. Aye, your horse, too. Start today."

So it was that Hywel—not Modron's husband but the deaf man who ran her byre—came to rely on Peretur. And by the third day Modron and her daughter, Angharad, and Hywel and his son, Rhodri, who sometimes listened and signed for him, would have been hard put to remember how they had managed without the stripling with the knack of calming horses, and around whom everything seemed a little better, a little easier. On the second day, when they were mucking out a stall, Rhodri took her into his confidence: He was to marry Angharad—"Angharad Ton Felen," he said in a voice filled with longing, Angharad of the Yellow Wave—it was quite understood. He would marry her now, today, but she said she was not yet ready.

And indeed Angharad, a lively young thing, paid more

attention to her customers than to Hywel's son, whom she treated with offhand kindness. She paid attention, too, to her mother, when she must. And then she began to pay attention to Peretur. At first it was the glance that lasted a little too long, and then standing close and resting a hand on a strong shoulder as she leaned to help Peretur add hay to the net in the stall. Then the long, searching look, the uncertainty, the hitch in her breath, breath that touched Peretur's cheek and told her of Angharad's longing to reach out, to touch, to taste her throat and, in turn, tip back her head and let her own throat be kissed. And Peretur, drawn like a horse to water, one day shifted a little closer, and let Angharad take her hand and turn it over in the shaft of light coming through the gap in the byre roof and stroke it, stroke it again like a cat, until Peretur felt herself rising to the touch, and Angharad slid her arm around Peretur's waist and whispered, "Kiss me."

Her lips were soft and plump as rain and Peretur wanted to plunge her hands deep into her golden yellow hair, deep under her skirts to the soft places beneath, and she could feel their hearts thundering like horses, like horses yoked and racing together, pulling towards the same goal, breath tearing in and out, in and out.

Angharad pulled back, breathing hard. She searched Peretur's face. "Whoever you are, Peretur, I would have you."

And Peretur, not knowing what else to do or how to explain, took Angharad's hand and placed it on her own belly, then, with a questioning look, lower, and when Angharad did not pull away, lower still, between her legs.

"Oh," Angharad said. "Oh." Then, her cheeks flaming like sunset, she put both hands on Peretur's waist, looked directly at her, and said again, slowly and clearly, "I would have you. I would have you now."

And they climbed into the hayloft and stayed for some time.

In the next few days they did this many times, and it was the finest week of Peretur's young life, and she could not hide it. Rhodri would watch the stripling whistle as he brushed the horses, and laugh out loud for no reason, and hear Angharad singing when she thought no one could hear, and he would look hurt and puzzled. The tide of life ran so strong in Peretur that she could not stop if she wanted to, and she did not want to, but it was her gift to soothe worries and calm nerves, so she soothed Rhodri.

Early morning of Harvest Day, Peretur was filling a bucket at the well, and swirling the water to and fro with her hand, half dreaming, when the lake sang to her, and today the lake's song was strong and insistent and it was for her. She felt she might fall in and never come out, and when a bird landed on her arm, as they sometimes did, and whistled, it took a while to make sense of the thread of worry woven into the notes, a thread that in words was a memory of mother and daughter talking as they shelled peas.

"—get hurt."

"He won't hurt me, Mam. Per is . . . not like other men."

Modron snorts. "Child, I have eyes."

"Oh." The sound of a river of peas pouring into a bowl. "Well, Rhodri doesn't."

"No, and what he doesn't know won't hurt him. But Peretur will hurt you—No, let me finish. He's kind, yes, but he will hurt you nonetheless, because he will leave. This is not his place. You've only to look at his eyes."

Angharad has a smile in her voice. "And they are such dreamy eyes."

"Oh, I'll grant you that."

"And did you know he has a sword? He showed it to me. It's old, and I think it would break if it hit anything, and he said only that he found it. But can you imagine Rhodri with a sword?"

"He will spoil you for Rhodri."

"Don't worry so. I know he won't stay, and Rhodri will. I'll be content with Rhodri when it's time but, oh, Mam, for now Per makes my heart sing! And more than my heart. He is surely destined for greatness. Any who can make a woman feel like that when he touches her so—"

"Enough!" But with a laugh in her voice. "Take your joy, then, child, just tell me no more about it, and don't say I didn't warn you."

Peretur took the bucket to the kitchen, where the women were now chopping vegetables and affected to pay him no more mind than a carrot or half an onion.

An hour later she was at the well again, filling buckets for the horses, but this time avoiding the water, for she could feel fate thick in the air, when she heard horses jingling to a halt in the inn yard and three men swinging themselves down, slapping their leathers free of dust.

Modron called out, "Per! He's my best lad, your honours.

He'll see you right. Per! Ah, there you are. Tend their lord-
ships' horses and tell Hywel to keep their tack aside in the special stall. Now my lords, if you'll follow me I'll set you up with
the finest ale, served by the fair hand of my own daughter."

And Peretur found herself looking at the backs of Cei,
Bedwyr, and Andros as they walked away. The Companions of Arturus king, whom they called Artos, the bear. After a week listening to village talk, she knew something of
his most trusted men: Llanza—Lance—was a special friend;
Cei, his reeve; and Bedwyr, Andros, and Geraint—the egg-
shaped man—his counsellors.

She led the horses one by one to stalls in the byre. They
were fine beasts. She lifted off the saddle with the yellow-
and-green leather, and ran her hand along the bay gelding's
flank. Cei was still an uneasy rider. The old scar there spoke
to her of a rider kicking his mount at a thorn hedge, forcing
it to obey, and riding on, not noticing the blood for an hour.
Not a cruel man, not deliberately, but hot-tempered and jeal-
ous of his pride. One by one as she touched them, the horses
nudged her hands with their velvet noses; she scratched
them in just the places no one thought to scratch them; she
found the burr in the tail of Andros's fine-boned stallion
that had been bothering him for days. Bedwyr's mare was
like Bedwyr himself: friendly, reliable, earnest. And when
the horses were eating and half dreaming in their stalls, she
carried the gear to the side aisle where special wooden trestles were built. Hywel was not there, so she got out the cloths
and brushes and began to clean it piece by piece.

She had never seen such good leather: tight-pored and

fine-grained, supple, well-shaped, and beautifully dyed. The metal rings were perfectly formed of uniform width and thickness, and the saddles had hanging flaps, notched with holes to vary length, with leather-and-metal loops hanging from them. What were they for?

"Don't play with the stirrup, boy." Bedwyr, leaning against a post, arms folded, voice easy.

"Stirrup?" She let it drop, stood back, looking at it. Ah, for the feet. "They're new."

Bedwyr stopped leaning. "How did you know?"

Because you did not have them when you rode through Ystrad Tywi in spring. But she could not say that. "I have never seen such things."

"What's your name, boy?"

"Per." She deepened her voice a little. "Peretur."

He came closer. "I know you, I think."

"No, lord." He was looking at her too hard; his eyes were startling against his dark skin, like burnished bronze, glowing and greening in summer sun. She remembered to use the rougher-edged words of the common folk. "I'm new come to this village."

"You look . . . Well, for someone new, Peretur, Modron thinks well of you." When Peretur found nothing to say, he shrugged. "I will just take a look at Lél before I go. Last week her off foreleg felt hot, and I would see how it is after today's run."

"There is nothing wrong with her leg, lord."

"Is there not?" Bedwyr said. "Still, I would see for myself."

He did, running his hands along the mare's legs, then

stroked her glossy coat, fingered her brushed tail, and did the same for the other two mounts. "And this was all your work? Just you, in this short time?"

"Yes, lord."

He looked keenly at Peretur. "We've business just now with the farmers and local headmen, but when you're done, come find me. Good work deserves fair reward, and we've need of a good byre boy in Caer Leon."

⟡

IN THE HAY loft Peretur smiled as she stroked Angharad's hair and listened to her talk of Arturus's men—who were not happy, she said.

"Not happy?"

She nodded against Peretur's shoulder. "Especially the king's reeve. He didn't like being told the harvest was not as good as he'd hoped, or that there won't be enough blades made because with bandits about there's a lack of charcoal. I thought he was going to pick up the table and beat Afan the smith with it."

"And the others?"

"They're not happy, either, though more courteous about it. Mind, it seems to me there was some shadow on them even before news of the harvest. So you might want to wait a day or two to claim any reward."

Peretur shook her head. Today was the day, she could feel it.

Angharad sat up and brushed back her hair. "They'll be done with talk by now and wanting a drink. So I'm away. If you must come today for your reward, wait a while. Men, I have found, are more generous when their bellies are full."

So Peretur took her time brushing the straw from her hair. She drew on her best green breeks, *hurr*ed on the blade of her knife, rubbed it against her tunic, and looked at her reflection in the metal, one eye at a time. She smiled. Oh yes. Today was her day.

⟋⟍⟍

SHE HEARD THE laughter before she entered, mean laughter: Cei, legs stretched before him, hooting at Rhodri, who was just picking himself up from the floor. "You should look where you're going instead of mooning after the maid." He took a pull of ale, then thumped his leather cup on the board. "It's empty, lass." He looked lazily at Rhodri, standing hunched, then at Modron, and was about to say something malicious when Angharad slid between him and them and poured a thin, expert stream of ale into the cup.

"Wait," he said to Angharad without taking his eyes off Rhodri. "Byre boy, let me give you advice. If you want a girl, this is how you do it." And he slid his arm around Angharad's waist, pulled her to him, and kissed her.

Angharad's slap cracked around the room like a whip. Modron sucked in her breath. No one moved.

Cei, white skin showing a palm-sized red stain, pulled back his hand—but before anyone else could breathe or speak, Peretur had that hand in her own; firm, unmoveable. "No."

Disbelieving silence. "What did you say, boy?"

Angharad edged away, out of reach. Peretur let go of Cei's hand and stepped back a little. "You may not hit this woman."

"May not? *May* not? Oh, now, boy, now you will learn a lesson." He drew his sword.

Peretur was aware of Angharad tugging Rhodri away, leaving the room, but she kept her eyes on the sword.

"Cei," Bedwyr said. "Leave it. He's just a boy, a fool for love."

"Save your other cheek for the priests, brother. But don't worry. I will only thrash some respect into the boy."

"You will not," Peretur said, every word clear as glass. A Companion of the king to hit an unarmed woman . . .

And now Cei smiled, a wide genial smile. "For that, boy, and for aping your betters, you will bleed. But first you will kneel and call me lord, and I may let you choose which hand to keep."

"Cei," Bedwyr said, sharper now, and Peretur heard the worry, that Cei's pride had driven him beyond reason. Everyone in the room edged to the walls, but she watched the sword. She felt the weight of it in Cei's hand, felt his intent ripple down his arm, to the hand, to the hilt, to move the tip gently this way, then that, golden summer light running like oil down its fine edge and shimmering on the snake steel. A wide blade, double-edged, and short. A sword for thrusting.

But she felt strong and fine, and her fate was upon her. "Lord, they call you. But does a lord beat an unarmed woman? Does a lord threaten one who defends that woman?"

The air slowed, the light on the sword now flowing lazy

as a wave, and a column of midges caught in a slant of sunshine darned the air in a stately dance.

She watched Cei form the thought and the sword begin to draw back, back—a contemptuous draw, a draw from a lord facing a clumsy byre boy—and behind her a high call, strange and stretched, an undulation of golden hair, then a dark line turning and tumbling through the air, a solid line with silver at its tip.

Her sword, still in its scabbard; thrown by Angharad. She watched its lazy tumble, then reached, plucked it neatly from the air, and brought it, still sheathed, down on Cei's sword, down so hard it trapped the thrusting blade in its leather and wood. With a twist she wrenched the blade from Cei's hand like a stick, and it clattered on the floor.

They all stared at it for a moment, then Bedwyr stooped and picked it up. Cei stood, holding his arm, disbelief silencing him as cleanly as a sack over his head.

And now Angharad was by Peretur, golden head coming only to her collarbone, holding her belt with two hands, shaking where she stood. She spat at Cei. "This boy is a man. Twice the man you are. He is kind where you're cruel, he is strong where you're weak, and he knows full well how to make a girl *want* to be got, and to get her. And when he does he can last long, longer, I wager, than you! He is Peretur Paladr Hir, and he is destined for greatness!"

Bedwyr stepped in front of Cei, facing Peretur and Angharad, blocking Cei's view of them. "It's best that you leave now."

Peretur stayed rooted. "Lord, good work deserves good

reward, you said. And I claim my reward. I would come with you to Caer Leon, to Arturus king."

"Cei is the king's reeve, boy, and more. He would make life in the king's byre a misery."

"Not to work in the byre, lord. To fight."

Behind Bedwyr, Cei laughed. At first with the wild loose laughter of a man unsure of what is real, but slowly the laugh gathered to itself and became the laugh of a lord amused by a fool. "Do you think Artos will take any baker, byre boy, or butcher who wants to join the Companions, Peretur Hardspear? We are champions, boy, every one. And who are you? A byre boy with no name but one given by a country lass boasting of her country oaf's prowess in the hay. When you come to the king's general and offer your sword, the general will look at you and see a byre boy with no horse, no armour, and none to speak for him. None who count. The general— and I am that general, boy—will say, *You will never serve the king as long as there is breath in my body.*" And he took his sword back from Bedwyr, shouldered aside a man who did not move quick enough, and left.

Peretur stood in the middle of a room, holding an old sword with a gashed scabbard, not understanding what had happened.

Modron laid a hand on his arm and said sadly, "You'll be leaving, boy."

"Leaving?" But she had won.

"You'll have till tomorrow to make your goodbyes, but the first hour after dawn you'll be on your way." And she took Angharad firmly by the shoulders and steered her from the room.

Bewildered, Peretur looked at Bedwyr, who nodded. "The village depends on Caer Leon. Without Caer Leon's favour, the village—this inn, the byre, all of it—would dry up and blow away. If you stay, Caer Leon's custom will not. I'm sorry for it, for there's something about you that reminds me . . ." He shook his head. "But you must leave."

"I would take some reward."

Bedwyr looked disappointed but reached for his purse.

"It's not your gold that I want."

"Then what?"

She wanted time to reel itself back to the morning then reel out again, rightly, the way it should have, the way it was fated. "I want your good word. Speak for me."

"But Cei's right, boy. We don't know you. I can't speak for one I don't know, whose deeds I don't know. My counsel? Go make a name."

"But how?"

"Find those who matter, and get their good word." He voice became encouraging. "You're big, you're strong, and you move well—I've not seen Cei disarmed like that since Llanza first came. And you have a sword." He nodded at the battered thing in Peretur's hand. "Though I see it's a bit worse for—" His gaze sharpened. "Where did you get that?"

"It's mine."

"Unless I'm much mistaken it belonged to another. A friend." He put a hand on his knife. "Tell me where you got it. Tell me now."

"I found it in the snow by a dead man—long dead. He died in a fall from his horse, all alone." She remembered again that smoky, fuming accent. "He was your friend? What tongue did he speak?"

"He was a Pict, from far in the north, beyond the wall. Beyond even the second wall. And I would know how you knew he was not a Briton."

Peretur could not explain. "I found his spears, too. And a ring, carved with the device on his shield. The one you took back from the bandits."

"How—" Bedwyr stared. "It was you! You who saved Cei's life." He laughed softly and took his hand off his knife. "And with Talorcan's boar spear. Boy, why didn't you say so? Why didn't you make yourself known? Who are you, where are you from?"

After a moment Peretur said, "I have his ring still. It should go to his friend."

Bedwyr did not seem to hear him. "I told him not to go alone to Ystrad Tywi."

Peretur nodded. The valley was forbidding terrain for those who did not know it. "Why did he?"

"Um? Oh, a boast made at Eastermass after too much wine." He seemed to reach a decision. "The ring should go to his brother, Beli. No, not now: when you come back. When you come back with your name, and your full growth, then I will speak for you to Cei. And by then he might listen, for he can be a fair man. You've seen him disappointed, crossed, and at his worst."

She remembered Angharad's comments. "The farmers."

43

He nodded. "Though the farmers and their poor harvest are a small part of the whole. There is the king, too, who is raging and in need of counsel, but has none, for his chief counsellor and right hand, the wise man Myrddyn, is gone, and none know where. And meanwhile tithes are low, not only because of weather but through trouble of the king's own making—made against Cei's counsel, and mine, and Andros's. Defeated men might swear fealty, but desperate men have no honour."

"The bandits."

Bedwyr sighed. "Well-armed, organised bandits. Most were once honourable and hard-working, but in rising up for one lord against another, and being defeated, they have lost their place. Some try to go home, but when they arrive they find they are no longer the owner of that home. They find, instead, that to stay they must give service. They find it bitter, and the bitterness poisons them. They lose even that meagre place. And with no livelihood, they steal, and stealing becomes killing. Stealing and killing does something to folk, boy. They become careless of themselves and others, reckless with life they feel no longer has worth; they drink to excess, steal more than they need, kill more than they can eat, and become gluttonous wastrels with no pride. They are a plague on the land."

"But you can defeat them."

"We could. But the Companions have other charges, alliances to build with Gwynedd and the north, defences to build against the Eingl massing in the north and east with their axes and the Saessonin in the south with their stabbing-knives. And we are only so many." He stopped, shook his head. "Why do I tell you such things? But it is true. So go help the farmers. And when you have, when you have their good word, when you've grown out your muscles and grown in your moustaches, come back. I will speak for you then, Peretur Boarspear. And may fate be on your side."

WHEN SHE LEFT it was the last full swell of summer, when apples hung formed but still green from the trees. She wore her armour now openly, the sword at her side, and spears tied loosely and to hand. She rode Bony—less bony after two weeks in Hywel's byre and the gossip of his own kind—and her saddlebags were bursting with the fruit of the harvest, a gift of Modron, and a small handful of copper coin from Hywel. She wore a red briar rose at her shoulder, tucked there by Angharad after that last sweet and sleepless night.

"Red is your colour," Angharad had said, and kissed her on the cheek. "I will think of you always this way."

And Peretur knew it was a goodbye-and-we-are-done, so there was sad mixed with the sweet, but not much, for now she followed a clear path: make her name; Arturus at Caer Leon; and the lake of light.

There were no bandits close to Caer Leon. She moved outwards, from one farmstead to another, working, helping, listening. Apples were blushing and weighing heavy on the trees when she came to a farm lately visited by bandits who had stolen their prize heifer and calf. That night as she oiled her sword by the fire, listening to the tales, she offered to bring the calf and heifer back. The farmer laughed, then saw how sweetly the sword slid into its scabbard, and paused. After a look at his wife, and a scratch at his chin, he gave a cautious yes. Peretur smiled and they clasped on it. She set out the next day.

She found the bandits' clearing easily enough, for they smelled of boast and fear and self-hatred. Bedwyr had been right: their hearts were filled with bitterness.

At the clearing it was a hard fight: two men, two women, and a youth, armed with cudgels and knives, a scythe and an axe. Bony took a cut to his withers, and Peretur a ragged slash to her shoulder, and another—that she found later—across her ribs. She found, too, that a sword needed a tip to be a sword, but she killed two men and one of the women. With the second woman and the youth something stayed her hand, some faint scent, still, of flowers and wholesome air; she roped the last woman and the youth together and made them dig a grave for their dead in the centre of the clearing. While they dug she gathered their heap of weapons, a thin and abused ass, and the heifer—now with infected teats and no calf. After they filled in the graves, they dragged all the vile clothes and bedding on top of the mounds, broke down the makeshift lean-to they had used as shelter, and set the whole on fire. As it burned she looked at the woman and the youth. "And what should I do with you?" They had no answer. She rode with her spoils back to the farmer.

Most of the tools were useless but the scythe and axe were sturdy, and in exchange the farmer agreed to give Peretur food for a week. The farmwife, though, was most pleased about the ass, and the heifer, which could be nursed back to health.

"And these two?" she said, looking the woman and youth up and down as she had the heifer and ass. "I could make use of them."

Peretur considered them: ragged, sullen, and stinking, both looking fixedly at their feet. "You'd trust a bandit who doesn't even keep herself clean?"

The farmwife folded her arms and looked at Peretur as though she had just sprouted wings. "And how do you suppose a woman and young lad surrounded by wicked men and hunted like dogs by honest ones might keep themselves clean?" She shook her head, as though reading Peretur's thought: *But I kept myself clean.* "But what would a great lump of a man with a sword and spear know of fear?"

Peretur stared. It had never occurred to her that anything in the world might be a danger to her.

"Turn them over to me for a half-year and you'll see. I've plenty of work for them. And regular food, whole clothes, and a few nights sleep'll work wonders."

They might kill you, she thought. But no; if she believed that they would already be dead. "What if they escape and make more mischief?"

"Escape?" She looked amused. "Where to? You," she said to the youth. "Would you run off?"

He muttered something. It was hard to tell what because half his teeth were missing.

Peretur turned to the woman, who lifted her gaze at last. Her eyes were wide-spaced, dull as mud. "'E said no."

"And you?"

"Not if we'm food and straw to sleep on and none to pester and paw us in the night."

Peretur tasted the despair in her words, the bone-bleaching fear of her recent life: starving, running, terrified, cold, always hunted, nowhere to rest, even—especially—from her own band. This pitiful pair could not survive alone without banditry; nor could they survive banditry itself. They would be dead in a week. So fragile to be so feared by folk.

After that it did not take long. They all agreed to a half-year's bond, then the farmer's byre hand took them to the trough to wash. The farmwife bound Peretur's shoulder—she would not let her at her ribs, but took a little honey to spread on the cut later, though she knew she likely would not need it—and when that was done, and everyone well pleased, she asked of the farmwife and her husband three things: that they remember her name, Peretur, and be prepared to give their good word if asked; that they be willing to give the two bandits back if she came this way again in the spring; and that before moving on she might take a day to rest and eat and tend to Bony. To this they agreed most willingly, and said, too, they would pass the word to neighbouring farms and prepare the way.

As the days cooled, she got very good at knowing from a frank look to the eye, or a taste of honesty in a swing, when to hold the killing stroke and demand a half-year's bond on oath to offer to the wronged farmers as recompense. Honesty and frankness did not mean the captured bandits were fine folk, or kind, only that they might not murder another in their sleep. If they fell back into their old ways, then their bond holders would judge them afresh.

Even as she became good at knowing who should live, she grew even better at killing, able to hear in the rustle of a turning leaf the hint of a body turned sideways, mallet raised, waiting for her to pass; she felt in the brush of a wasp's wing the curdled heart of a woman who had killed another's child from spite; and she sensed in the shadow of a stave how a foot might move back unexpectedly and change the path of a blow. At those times, more often than not, she left the sword in its scabbard and used instead her javelin, boar spear, and knife. She was fast and without mercy, hurling the javelin hard enough to split a sapling and pierce the man behind it; using blade and shaft and weighted foot of the boar spear; and edge, tip, and haft of her knife. By the time the acorns began to harden to brown, farmers had begun to send messages to her, pleas to rid their heath or valley or wood of bandits. And in one low smoky longhouse of a village headman, where folk of many steadings had gathered to swap kine before winter and found they each knew of her deeds, she was once again named Peretur Paladr Hir, though this time in earnest: Peretur Hardspear, Peretur Bitterspear, Peretur Spear Enduring. In that same steading she found a smith who added a razor edge to all her blades, but who refused to try to add a tip to Talorcan's sword. Work for a king's smith, he said; work for a royal armourer.

It was from this smith that she first heard of the Red Knight.

Once a lord of the neighbouring valley, the Red Knight had risen against the king; the Companions defeated his warband and drove him out. Now he was back, demanding tithes of any folk crossing the main ford of the Redcrest road that ran east to Caer Gloiu. And now he tithed not as lord, taking a small portion in exchange for protection and justice, but as a thief, taking what he wanted and offering in return only fear. Local farm men had banded together in summer and tried to take him, but he was a lord, well-mounted and well-armed; he killed three of their number and hung them from the tree by the ford. The farmers then sent to Caer Leon but were told: *Perhaps in spring.*

PERETUR RODE NOW through lands abandoned by people and sharp with the scent of vinegar where apples, unpicked, had fallen and rotted in the grass. A good land, and rich, but poisoned by fear.

Midway across a cold, clear stream she caught the thick scent of corruption, and stopped. She loosened the reins. "Drink deep, Bony. Drink your fill." There might not be much ahead that was good and clean.

On the far bank she drank to bursting, then filled her leather bottle. She gave Bony the last beans mixed with oats, then turned him loose to graze the paling autumn grass while she ate what she could, and saw to her gear. The blades were sharp, sharper than sharp, and well-oiled, but she oiled them again, even the pointless sword. She checked her mail coat, scale by scale, and put it back on; tied, untied, and adjusted the laces until her great veins were covered but she could still move well. The cap she turned over in her hands. It was a little tight now, but the smith had reinforced the ear flaps and added one for the neck. She might wish Bony were bigger, and she might wish for a shield, but this was what she had.

IN YSTRAD TYWI, close to the bounds of Dyfed, there was a blackthorn where shrikes spiked their prey—mouse pups, caterpillars, smaller birds, bees—a score of dead things drying to husks, hanging as a larder and a warning.

The Red Knight had hung more.

Bare alders, and willows still clinging to their leaves, grew on both sides of the ford, and the crook of every bough held remains. Men, women, even children. Two dogs. A goat. Half an ass. And that was just the carcasses fresh enough to recognise. There were more, many more, that had rotted into strips of leather and old bone held together by a piece of armour, a boot, or a sleeve. It would be the work of a week to bury it all.

In the dappled light on the far bank, mounted on a giant roan, waited a man cased in red leather sewn with red-enamelled scales: not just a mail coat, like the old thing Peretur wore, but also plate strips on his breeches, a high iron collar, and gauntlets sewn with small plates on each finger. Even his boots were plated. The shield on his left arm was matching red leather stretched over wood and painted with a black snake with golden eyes and tongue; around its edge another snake, this time of armoured scales, glinted in the shimmering tree light. Boiled leather covered his horse's chest, face, and neck. The man had a massive war helm of red-enamelled iron, a big two-handed sword sheathed on the left of his saddle, and a great lance tucked under his right arm.

Peretur patted Bony's shoulder and could not tell if her horse trembled or she did. Was this fear? She felt once again Angharad's breath on her cheek—*Red is your colour*—and that first cool kiss of the dream lake. The lake was her destiny; her path to it lay through this knight.

She forced her war hat more firmly on her head and wished suddenly to see her valley again, see it on one of those precious sunlit days when forget-me-nots lay scattered blue in the grass and the light on the leafed-out trees glowed like polished bronze. For a moment, in a shiver of sunlit leaf shadow, she almost remembered something, but then a fly lifted from the giant lance and hummed over the water, and, in the air stirred by its wing, she felt the strength of the arm that held that lance and the speed with which it could change the direction of the brutal tip—an edged blade as much as a point.

With nothing in her hands but Bony's reins, she kneed him forward. The Red Knight's horse overtopped her own by two hands; Bony would not survive a blow to his head or neck from those plate-sized forehooves. And that shield . . .

She took a deep breath. "I am Peretur Paladr Hir!" She used her lungs, large from years of running the valley, and her gut muscles, and her voice boomed and bayed like a huge hound. "In the name of Arturus king, your life is forfeit!"

With Bony's first step into the river the knight's memory of sharpening the scales around the shield rim unfurled in her mind like a scroll. When the knight kicked his own giant mount forward, its tail flicked an alder at the water's edge, and she knew from the scent of its bark that, hidden from sight, another two spears were propped against its trunk, waiting.

She kicked Bony into a trot and he splashed water high around him in a brave show, and, with her knees holding him steady, she pulled out her boar spear, which she tucked under her left arm, then her javelin, which she held easy in her right.

She swayed with Bony, loose and lithe as the river, while the bandit knight bore down on her like a red tide. He was ferment and rot wearing the gear of a prince and lord, a wave of blood and rage. *Send me strength,* she called—to whom?— kicked Bony to a gallop, and hurled her javelin hard and true. It took the shield near its edge and swung it into his lance, nudging it out of true, just as she and Bony swept past inside the reach of the Red Knight's blade—close enough to feel the wind of the shield as it missed—then swerved and thrust her boar spear at his thigh. And they were past.

Both horses turned. Peretur wiped her jaw: blood, dripping down her cheek; the red shield had not quite missed. She put it from her mind. The knight shook his shield but the javelin had burst through leather and wood, and was unmoveable. He threw it down in the shallows along the water's edge—the javelin stood upright like a sapling growing from the river—and kneed his mount into a tight turn.

He was bigger, his mount was bigger, his lance was bigger, and he knew this river. She could not win.

But as he came, Peretur felt, through her palm, the wood of her spear; from the wood, the blade; and, at the tip of the blade, a taste of blood—not much blood, for she had barely pricked him—but enough: for now she could feel his life, feel the Red Knight as she felt herself. Now his knowledge was her knowledge. She felt his belly tighten as he lifted his lance a fraction and knew he planned to lower the point and take Bony in the lung; she felt the movement of his eyes as he searched for, and found, the telltale runnel of water where a shallow tree root lay hidden to trip the unwary.

Even as she felt it, she lifted Bony to a jump, up, over the root, and pulled her tipless sword free. As his lance point dropped she slashed down, taking off both blade and a handspan of shaft just before it slammed into Bony and sent him crashing down in the water. She leapt free, waist deep, boar spear in one hand and sword in the other, and as the knight thundered past she swung again, hard, high up along the shaft of his lance, leaving him holding a stub. He tossed the stub aside and spurred his horse for the bank—for the tree and the hidden spears.

She could not move fast against the weight of water, not against a mounted man, so she did the only thing she could and hurled the boar spear across the horse's path, straight into the bank. The roan caught its leg and went down.

The Red Knight rose, a red raw mountain, rose and drew his sword from the scabbard on the saddle of the thrashing horse.

They stood opposite each other, she to her waist in the water, he with his back to the bank and only to his knees in the shallows. She moved on a slant closer to the bank, to where he knew—as now did she—that the riverbed sloped up towards the grass. Now she was only thigh-deep. They faced each other and the sun shone full on the bandit knight's face. His eyes were glass green, almost wholly green, with centres tight as pinpricks.

"I will hang you," he said in a voice harsh as gravel. "I'll hang you alive, pinned by your own spear, but not through anything vital. I'll eat your horse while you watch. And every day I'll cut a piece from you and laugh as you rot and beg to die." And he waded towards her.

She could do nothing but watch him come. She felt the power of his muscle against the weight of water, saw the length and weight of his sword, knew the strength of his armour—armour on his throat and chest and arms and belly and thighs. Her sword could not stab through that armour; it had no point. She would die, hanging on his tree. Her legs trembled. She could not stand against him—

So she did not.

As the wake of his travel washed against her and that great sword drew back for a scything cut that would take an arm, or her head, she breathed deep and dived flat—under the water, under his blow—and slid the edge of her blade across the inside of his knee, where a riding man never wore armour, could not wear armour. He stumbled to one knee and she pulled her broken but razor-sharp—oh, sharper than sharp!—sword back along the inside of the other knee, slicing it open, deep, to the bone. He fell sideways and she pushed herself up, breathing hard, to one knee and one foot—the foot on his sword, trapping his blade—and thrust her own, pointless sword down against his chest, pushing him under. As she got her feet under her, she shifted, and lifted her sword, and thrust down again, this time on the collar across his throat. She leaned her whole weight on the blunt and broken blade, leaned and leaned, gasping, holding on while he thrashed, holding on even as the water turned red around him and he went still, holding on even as she sank, exhausted, to her knees, still holding, still leaning, until Bony, limping, nosed the back of her neck and she fell against him, weeping, the blood running down her face mingling with blood from the ragged tear on Bony's chest and running, with the river, away.

ONE DAY IN spring, just past noon, a knight in red arms and red leather mounted on an armoured red roan rode into a village near Caer Leon. The knight led a scarred, bony horse burdened with bundled weapons, and was followed by a score of farmers on an assortment of ponies and carts, mules and asses leading a great gaggle of men and women braceleted in rope, though it was loose rope, and the village folk who came out to gawp saw that those who were bound did not seem much restrained by their bonds. The cavalcade did not stop but rode on, through the village, slowing only when the knight passed the byre and inn where a woman with beautiful yellow hair stood, and the young man next

to her put a protective arm around her waist. The knight raised a gauntleted hand, and the woman saw the bony gelding and smiled, but the knight rode on.

The children ran after the strange group for half a mile. They soon tired, as children do, but one villager rode ahead, and when the knight and his group came to the double-walled fort of Caer Leon the gates were shut and the palisade crowded with men.

The knight reached for a red shield with its sigil painted out and settled it on a mailed left arm.

"Who comes to the gate of Caer Leon with an unmarked shield?" called the door warden in a sun-scented accent from the walk above the gate.

"One with business with Cei, reeve and general to Arturus king."

"And what do you want with Lord Cei?"

"I bring him a challenge." A byre boy could not challenge a lord Companion, but a well-armed, well-armoured, well-mounted man speaking the language of high folk, and with two score followers, could.

Silence, followed by low voices.

Then a man in blue-and-brown leathers stood tall next to the lushly bearded door ward and called, "And why should the king's general accept the challenge of a knight who paints out his sigil?"

"Say, rather, of a knight who would fight for Arturus king with no proof of their worth but deeds. Here, as token of my worth, are a score of bandits-become-bondsmen, willing to work for one year for their king; tools and weapons no longer turned against the farmers who feed the king's folk; and the good word brought by those farmers whose troubles I have soothed."

More conversation, some of it sharp and aimed at someone out of sight below.

The gate creaked open. The door ward called, "Send in your tokens, Sir Red. On behalf of Lord Cei, Lord Bedwyr bids you climb down from your horse, rest, and refresh yourself as you await Cei's answer."

The farmers, leading the bondsmen, looked at the knight, but the knight gave no sign so they stayed where they were.

Then the man in blue-and-brown leathers came through the gate leading two servants laden with food, stools, trestles, and a board; he carried a bucket and a nosebag.

"If you won't come in and eat, Sir Red, then you and I will eat out here. Here is food for you, and for your horse. Horses. For all know how you value your mounts." He grinned, and winked one of those startling greened-bronze eyes. "But send in your proofs meanwhile so that Cei may judge for himself. And we will talk, you and I."

AS BEDWYR HAD predicted over food, Cei chose to fight on foot. He stood now at the centre of a crescent of Caer Leon folk to the west side of the gate, skin winter pale in the spring sun, shield on his left arm, short stabbing sword sheathed at his waist, and helm held loosely in his right hand. Opposite him, at the centre of a crescent of farmers and village folk who had followed in their own time to the fort—for

Angharad had told them who wore the red armour—stood Peretur already helmed, red leather cheek flaps laced so tight that all that was visible was the tip of a scar running over the cheekbone past the outer edge of her left eye. She carried no shield, and instead of a sword held a red-painted boar spear.

The challenge will be to first blood or to yield, Bedwyr had said. *Cei is good and he can fight with either hand. He likes to stay close to the ground and come up under your guard. And he will taunt you to get you to attack first.*

"Afraid to show your face?" Cei called. "Is it hideous?" He pulled on his helm and crouched, holding the shield before him and the short sword only a foot beyond that. "Will the maids run screaming when I unhelm you?"

Peretur said nothing. Cei was trying to nudge her to the north and east so the slanting afternoon sun would strike her eyes. Behind her cheek flaps she smiled.

Cei's shield was heavy; she could see the ridge of his arm muscle as he moved it. She studied it as he moved forward, one pace, two. She backed away, watching. He was buckled into it, not merely gripping. He would not swap sword arms.

"Ah, ugly and afraid." Silence. "Dumb, too? I will make you scream, country knight, scream like a lamb in the jaws of a wolf."

Metal, she realised. Beneath the leather of his shield was a thin sheet of iron or bronze, enough to turn most thrown spears. Enough to trap a thrust spear. She ignored the shield.

Cei ran at her. She saw the moment he expected her to flinch with the sun in her eyes and stepped swiftly to one side, polished spear blade tilted just so, and the sun's light ran over her blade and leapt into his eyes instead. She could have taken him then, slid her spear blade over his shield and into his throat, cored him with a twist and a flood of blood. But this was a challenge, not a hunt; and she had no intention of killing the king's general.

She waited, content to circle. The wind veered from south to northwest, from the fort and beyond the fort.

Cei called more taunts, but she was smelling the wind and no longer listening. The wind brought her news of Bony, revelling in good rich hay, munching complacently as a byre girl traced the ragged but healing scar over his chest muscles where the Red Knight's broken spear had taken him down. And from beyond the byre, beyond Caer Leon's wall, the scent of the lake, wide and deep and waiting. And on the edge of the lake, a woman's hand, running through it, over it, pushing gently, testing the surface as she might a lover's taut belly. And almost Peretur could hear the words, a song of—

Cei came roaring at her, and she stepped forward and past his stab, listening, listening for that—

Another roar, and, impatient now, Peretur swung the weighted butt of her spear up, cracked it smartly under Cei's chin, and, in a fluid reverse, swung the spear blade over and down, hard and flat, against his sword arm. The sword went flying and Cei fell in a heap on top of his shield.

But the scent of the lake was gone.

Peretur blinked. Cei was struggling to roll himself off his shield, and could only get himself to his knees, leaning his weight on the shield, right arm hanging limp. He bent and with his teeth unbuckled the shield, which he let drop.

"By the breath of Arawn!" He pulled off his helm left-handed. "You've a strong arm! You're welcome to Caer Leon, Sir Red, and more than welcome. But I would know your name."

Peretur reached out her left hand and hauled Cei to his feet. Then she pulled off her helm. "Peretur."

Cei stared at her, then burst out laughing. "Byre boy!" He laughed again, good strong laughter with no twist beneath it. "Peretur the Hard, Peretur the Enduring, Peretur Longspear! And grown even taller, I see, though still with no moustaches—all the better to show off that handsome scar, no doubt. I don't know what spell you cast on that poor girl—but you had me fooled, too, talking like a country oaf! Imagine me thinking you were a byre boy!" He tried to shrug then hissed in pain. "But, Peretur Everlasting, did you really have to break my arm?"

"It's not broken. Though it will hurt for a while." And, grinning, they clasped each other by the left arm, broke apart, and then were swarmed by Companions—Bedwyr, and Andros, and many others, whose names she would learn in time—who slapped her on the back and made jokes about her name, for clearly they knew the story of the byre boy who had disarmed the king's general with an unsheathed sword in an argument over a girl. Others, including Llanza, only watched, but she did not care. She was here, at last. Here, where she belonged.

After a while, Cei dragged Peretur to the trough. "Wash

the dust off, lad. You wanted to be a Companion? Come meet the king."

〰️

IT WAS NOTHING like the stories. No king and queen arrayed in glittering gold, no roaring fire or men beating time to bard song, no boasts or toasts over wine. It was a man and a woman sitting at a table at one end of the echoing hall, and the fire was out, for it was spring, and there was no wood to waste, and they were there to listen to their captains and counsellors, to hear news and take reports, to tally supplies and make plans.

There was food at the table, good food but plain, and the cups were made of wood, though those Arturus and Gwenhwyfar drank from were beautiful turned maple, with chased silver rims. Llanza was there, with Andros, and another man.

"I bring you our latest recruit!" Cei shouted to them as they entered. "Pour me a cup of that, Lance, and one for the mighty Peretur here." He clapped Peretur on the shoulder, then straightened. "Artos, my king, and Gwenhwyfar, my queen, allow me to present Peretur Paladr Hir, terror of the lawless." Then he grinned. "Not even full-grown and already a match for your general."

Gwenhwyfar's hair was so pale as to be almost white. Her eyes were pale, too, though pale hazel—much paler than Bedwyr's—the greenish gold of almost ripe wheat; a woman like a great hunting owl, soft-winged, silent, strong-taloned. There was no wind in the hall, no fly to land on Gwenhwyfar's hand and tell Peretur all she needed—and she could read nothing into the queen's carefully judged smile. Arturus's hair was black as the Dagda's midnight stallion, his shoulders wide and his arms great; she understood how he got the name Bear. His eyes were hooded so deep in their sockets she could not at first tell what colour they were. But she was not looking hard, because she had eyes only for the sword at his side, which drew her so strongly she had to use half her attention to not reach out to the silvery hilt.

"So, what do you think? Artos?"

Peretur dragged her gaze away from the sword. She met Arturus's gaze briefly, and in that moment did not need a breeze or a fly to tell her what he felt: distrust, dislike, disdain. Why?

Cei, too, seemed puzzled. He looked from his king to his friend. "Lance?"

But it was the man next to him, fingering a knot in the elmwood table, who stirred and spoke. "You are the one who found my brother's body."

His words smoked and fumed with the same accent as her memory of Talorcan. "I did, my lord Beli. He was some months dead, from a fall. I gave his body all reverence. And"—she fumbled open her bright purse—"I bring you this." She stepped forward and put the worn coin and the ring by Beli's hand.

He picked up the ring, turned it in his hand, then looked at her, his eyes dark and sharp as apple pips. "Where did you find him?"

She described to him the valley, the snow that did not give like snow, his broken leg.

"And you took his arms and armour, like a common thief."

"I did not know his name. And he had no use for them."

"And you, Peretur." The queen's voice was supple but not soft. "Why were you there to find him? Who are your people?"

And Peretur could say nothing. She could not open her mouth and say, *My mother is Elen, and we lived in a cave,* because until that moment she had forgotten she had a mother, had forgotten the cave, and realised that even if she tried to say the words her mother's geas would turn her tongue to stone, for the cave, and Elen, and her treasure must stay hidden, always. She sought desperately for a way to speak.

"I did not know my father, lady." She bowed her head to hide the confusion, the grief, the rage—her own mother made her forget!—rising to her eyes. "We grew up with nothing." She glanced at Bedwyr, then Cei. "When Cei thought me a country oaf, he was not wrong."

Cei grinned and slapped her on the shoulder again, but no one at the table smiled.

She turned to Beli. "I have your brother's armour, also, and will bring it for you, though I warn you it is the worse for wear. Meanwhile—" She unhooked the scabbard at her side from its baldric, wrapped the ties around the sheath, and laid sword and sheath on the table. "Here is his sword. It's broken. I'm sorry."

Beli ran a hand down the battered sheath. "It was our father's," he said. "Broken off in the rib of the man who killed him. Talorcan swore never to mend it until he found our father's killer. I'll keep the ring, and I thank you for it, but the sword has brought me and mine nothing but grief." He pushed it back to Peretur.

For the first time, Llanza spoke. "The gash on the scabbard is, I think, new."

"I told you how that happened," Cei said. "I told you, too, lord." Arturus said nothing. "Are we going to keep this poor lad apologising until the Eingl and Saessonin come swarming over the wall? I want him under my command."

Arturus looked at Peretur as though looking at an enemy through his visor. "I take none into my Companions I don't know."

"But—"

Arturus silenced Cei with a look. He rested his palm on the pommel of his sword in what Peretur recognised not as a threat but the habit of a possessive man reassuring himself of his treasure. *Mine. This is mine and you may not have it.* "You bring the good word of not only the common folk but of people I trust." He nodded at Cei and Bedwyr. "Nonetheless, there is a feel to you that makes me uneasy, Peretur Paladr Hir. What might that be?"

The sword called to her, and somehow Arturus felt that.

"I would know where and who you're from."

She stood there helplessly, desperately seeking a way around the geas. "I never knew my father," she said again slowly. She could only tell the truth. "Of the rest, I may not speak."

"A vow?" Cei said. "A vow! Then all is well. For no one would hold you to a vow before the king."

"A vow is a vow," Peretur said.

"Oh, come now—"

But Bedwyr was nodding. "So that's why you couldn't announce yourself when you helped us with the bandits." He drew himself up. "Lord king. I speak now for this man. From the way he treats beasts and women I deem his heart good. I have seen him fight. I would gladly trust his right arm in battle. I speak for him. I say: Yes, we take him."

"Of course we take him," Cei said belligerently. "I'm your general, and I say yes. Andros?"

Andros nodded. "I was there in Ystrad Tywi. Perhaps I am here today because of Peretur Paladr Hir. Yes."

"Beli?"

Beli looked at the ring on his hand and closed his fist. "He honoured my brother. He returned to me not only the ring, but a coin that clearly he could have used. Yes."

"Lance?"

Llanza's brown eyes were troubled. "We don't know if what he tells of Talorcan is true, though my heart tells me it is. But there is something . . ." He opened his hands. "I don't know." He looked at Gwenhwyfar.

The queen rested her chin on her fist. She studied Peretur's face—jaw to hair, then eyes, and back to hair again. It was all Peretur could do to resist reaching up to see if there was something caught in it. Gwenhwyfar leaned back. "I also do not know. Perhaps."

Arturus looked directly at Peretur. His eyes were the blue-grey of good slate. "Those I love do not dismiss you out of hand, and by all accounts you have fought well in our name. But the Companions are mine to choose, mine to command. They are the heart of my strength, and I must be able to trust that strength." He shook his head. "Therefore, until you stand before all and speak of who named you, who reared you, my answer is no. But no man may call me ungenerous. I do not refuse you the hospitality of Caer Leon. You may stay a time."

He stood, as did Gwenhwyfar, and they left the hall. Llanza stood and said quietly to Peretur, "Tomorrow, before you break your fast, come find me." Then he followed the king and queen.

Peretur stood there while men clapped him on the shoulder or pressed a drink in his hand, or reassured him the king would change his mind; he was a good king, and fair. But Peretur had felt Arturus's refusal; his mind was set. It was like the village all over again: she had won, but still must leave. She could not bear it.

෯෧෧

IN THE GREY light just past dawn, Llanza showed her Caer Leon. It was a double fort: a smaller fortified place inside a larger, and thronged with people, more people than Peretur had ever seen in one place: two hundred armed men and twice that many other folk—smiths and farriers, bakers and weavers, messengers and leather workers; so many that even with only a few awake she kept herself closed to the sound and song and breath of life in the air, and used only her eyes, ears, and nose. In the inner fort was the king's hall and byre, lesser buildings for the Companions and their folk, for many had wives and, some few, children; there was a well, bread ovens, a granary, many small plots for fresh herbs, a still room, and food cellars dug deep in the dirt. A rooster crowed; a chicken, still half asleep, pecked; soon geese would waddle and the goats come pitter-pat to the midden to chew side by side, staring with their yellow, slot-centred eyes. A striped cat lounged on the roof of the granary, and somewhere she heard the yip of dreaming pups. Peretur had never seen so many beasts living in so small a space; even closed, if she shut her eyes she could hear them, feel them, taste their curiosity. In the vast space between the walls were the forge and smithy, workshops, the main byre and kennels. It was a good place, a fine place, and it should have been her place to belong. Only it was not; Arturus did not want her.

Here and there Llanza would pause his rolling limp and point out this or that. He stopped again just past the kennels—at rest he balanced his weight evenly between the straight right leg and the twisted left; it did not seem to hurt, and she guessed he had been born with it—and nodded at a strange wire coop low to the ground. No, not a coop, for it was bigger and did not smell of feathers.

"Coney," Llanza said. "Like hares, but smaller. Gwenhwyfar likes coney."

Coney. Even mostly closed, Peretur sensed them in their burrows beneath the wire, nothing much in their tiny minds but the need for warmth and safety among others of their kind—she envied them—with none of the wild cunning of hares. Soft-furred, soft as the note in Llanza's voice when he spoke Gwenhwyfar's name. She looked at him as they walked among the horses in the byre. His eyes were as liquid as run honey, dark clover honey, and his hair was a rich brown with bronze sun streaks, but his beard, like his eyebrows, was black. His face and hands were the colour of walnut, or perhaps elm bark, but lighter where his sleeves rode up above his wrists. He was not thick-boned and heavy-muscled like Cei, but whippy as a hazel rod, and she knew she would not face him lightly in battle.

"And Arturus? What does the king like?"

"Artos will like what Gwen likes, for her sake." That soft note was back again, the same for Arturus as for Gwenhwyfar. Perhaps she was mistaken in its meaning. "But for his own sake, he likes to hunt his meat with hound and hawk, ride the hills far from worry." No, she was not mistaken; she knew that note.

Now they came to Bony, who was dreaming with one leg hitched up. He woke and she gave him half a carrot from her pocket, showed Llanza the scar on his chest, described the fight as best she could, couching as luck the moments where she chose based on knowing what the Red Knight knew; but perhaps Llanza heard something missing, for he looked at her in the growing light.

"You are uncommon lucky, Peretur Paladr Hir. And so is your horse." He patted the bony gelding, then turned to the roan, a hand taller than any other in the byre. "This one, now. He is magnificent."

Peretur gave the roan, now Broc, the other half carrot and pointed out the thick scars on his flanks—the mark of cruel spurs—and the smaller scar on his right knee from a gash when he fell at her spear.

"And yet he comes to you like a lamb. You're lucky with animals, too, I see. Or perhaps it is not luck."

"I was born with a gift for animals." Llanza waited. Hoping she might say more about her birth? She tried. "In the wild, animals were my friends."

She saw from his softening face that he understood: she had had no other friends.

He patted his left leg. "I know what it is to feel . . . outside, even among my own. As a boy in Astur I was not good at the games of run and chase, and stick and ball. Even now, on foot I am ordinary with a sword. But I took to the saddle before most boys could run, and in the saddle, I'm told, I have no equal." He smiled slightly. "Or perhaps had no equal."

She stroked Broc's nose one more time.

"I hope you will stay long enough for us to one day put that to the test. But for that you will need patience. I've seen Artos take against someone so just once, and he's not a man who changes his mind easily. I admit I, too, had my own misgivings, for there is something uncanny about you. Will you speak of it?"

"I cannot." And her heart ached, because her mother, too had pushed her away, and bound her tongue so she could not even speak of it. They left the byre and moved towards the outer wall. "Had—you said you *had* misgivings. Not anymore?"

"You are . . . I don't know how, or why, but you're not as other men. Though perhaps that is not a bad thing. And, too, I've never known a horse to be wrong about the heart of a man. Dogs, though, oh yes. Dogs can be foolish beasts."

They both smiled, and Peretur felt a little less lonely, a little less lost.

Llanza nodded to the smithy. "Afan can put a tip on that sword of yours."

"I don't think the sword is my weapon."

"Well, he'll be there when you choose."

As they passed each gate in the outer wall, Llanza would say where it led—this one to a spring where they drew most of their water; that to the great east-west road to Caer Gloiu; the other to the high sheep pasture—but would have passed without comment a small gate to the northwest, more of a door than a gate, if Peretur had not stopped. "And this one?"

Llanza look surprised, as though he had not seen it. "Oh. That is Nimuë's gate. It opens for none without permission. It leads up into the folded hills, and the lady's lake."

"Nimuë," she said, tasting the name. Nimuë. And a lake. Her lake?

"With Myrddyn gone, she's Artos's chief counsellor. She's—"

Nimuë, chief counsellor to the king.

"—Myrddyn's pupil. And perhaps more than his pupil."

There was a lot he was not saying. Why did she live outside Caer Leon? "I would meet her. When will she come?"

Llanza clapped Peretur on the shoulder—very like Cei, only not so hard. "Don't think it, Per. She's subtle and not to be meddled with. But don't worry, there are plenty here who are already eager to find out if your name matches the truth." He grinned when Peretur turned pink. "But if you're not too busy fending off admirers, you'll meet Nimuë soon enough. She speaks with the king often."

⟨᷒᷒᷒⟩

AFTER SHE BROKE her fast, Peretur took her last oat cake to the walled kitchen garth. It had not been part of Llanza's tour—what fighting man would be interested in plants? But she was her mother's daughter, and there was nothing growing she did not want to know. And at the thought of her mother, whom she had forgotten again, she had to stop and catch her breath. Her childhood, her *life,* and she kept forgetting; her mother's geas kept taking it away. Then she was thinking of her mother, seeing her in the clearing on one of her good days, forget-me-not eyes dancing with light. *Mother?* She listened. Nothing.

She wiped her eyes, her not-blue eyes, and walked on through a drift of rain so fine it settled on her sleeve like dew.

She smelt it a hundred strides away—aged manure forked into dirt and heaped in rows—and as she drew closer she heard the sifting shift of soil, and was not surprised to find someone there before her. A woman, stooped and hooded against the mizzle, poking a hole with a stick with one thrust, dropping a seed; thrust, drop; thrust, drop. Early for a house worker. Then she caught the white-pale flash beneath the hood and stopped.

Gwenhwyfar straightened. "Peretur."

"Lady." She suddenly didn't know what to do with the oat cake in her hand.

"Bring me those," she said, pointing to the bundle of rods lying against the east wall.

Peretur stuffed the oat cake in her mouth, chewed furiously, and swallowed as she carried the rods. Gwenhwyfar was smoothing dirt over the seeds, and without needing to be told Peretur began setting the rods in a row to support the pea vines as they grew, pressing the dirt down firmly with her foot. It was good dirt, wriggling with pink rolls of worms, and dark with leaf mould. A spider trundled along and stopped, waved its front legs at her.

Gwenhwyfar was watching her.

Perhaps she was wondering what a knight wanted with a garden. She fought to speak, hauling up the words as though pulling a bucket of stones up a deep, deep well. "My m . . . My *mother* grew peas." It came out shockingly loud. My mother, my mother, my *mother*. She said it again. "My mother grew peas, my lady. Herbs and other greens are an interest of mine." And they fell to talking of whether it might be a dry summer or not—the rooks were nesting high; they did not expect storms—and perhaps they might plant the next row a little deeper against the drying heat of the sun.

They moved on to stripping dandelion leaves for tea. A mistle thrush sang, and Gwenhwyfar said, nodding to a fork in the apple tree against the north wall, "I fear for the seeds, but I haven't the heart to move the throstle's nest."

Throstle. Gwenhwyfar was not from Dyfed or Glywising or Gwent. "As a child I watched over seeds against the birds. My mother would never chase them from their nests. She said if we let them be, once the seeds had sprouted the thrush and her brood would repay us threefold. And she did. Our peas and cabbages were never eaten by caterpillars or ruined by fly eggs."

"And she is a peaceful companion." She sounded wistful, and Peretur understood that in her need for companionship she had disturbed what might be the queen's only daily peace, so she finished stripping leaves from her dandelion, bowed, and left.

☙❧

THE WORKSHOPS WERE opening. A yawning blacksmith's girl pumped half-heartedly on the bellows to wake the forge for the morning, and a youth drove half a dozen piglets towards the butcher's stall. Peretur left by the gate Llanza had said led to a spring, and followed a well-trodden path up into the westward hills.

She stopped before she got to the spring, at a lichened grey stone with a saddle-shaped top. She sat with the morning sun behind her left shoulder and stared west to the mountains where they rose with the fresh bright green of new grass, then darker with distance, then bluer, then blue-grey, then grey, then mist. Beyond them all lay the valley, and in the northwest of that valley, a thicket. And hidden in that thicket, her mother. *Elen.* Her mother Elen. There trees would be blossoming and leaf buds spilling mint lace at their tips; the peas planted in their sheltered clearing two weeks since and the shoots already reaching through the dirt to the light.

It was lovely here, and she was alone. Slowly and with care she relaxed, let her senses uncurl. She listened to the liquid ripple of blackbird song and let herself feel the rise and fall of its tiny breast; watched the scudding approach of cloud from the southeast and let herself feel the gathering of droplets within. She had her name, her good name. She was here in Caer Leon, and she had beaten the king's general in challenge. But still she had no home, and she was struck with yearning: to talk to her mother, the one who knew her best; to hear the little catch of her mother's voice when she called her Dawnged. She wanted more than anything to be Dawnged to her mother now: a gift, a blessing. She was tired of striving, tired of the sideways look of those who did not trust her. She wanted to belong; to sit before the hearth and dip soup from the hanging bowl, or sit cross-legged before her mother who perched on a stool that she, her daughter, had made, to hear Elen use her name, Peretur, with love while she combed through her gold-streaked brass hair; to pause, between sips, and tell her mother of Bony, her horse; of the queen who grew peas just like theirs; and of the soft little coneys warm together in their burrow.

Mother, she called, and listened. *Mother!* She listened again. Almost.

Out here, away from walls and shade trees, some dandelions were already ripe and going to seed. She bent and picked one, twirling the white puffed globe in her fingers.

Mother, she thought, and this time as she reached she pushed against a barrier like skin, soft, and then unyielding. She drew in a breath and closed her eyes, pushed harder, then pushed in one sharp stab, and punched through. *Mother, I am well. I am here. I am safe and cradled in the hand of fate.* And she blew, one long breath, sending the seeds purling into the wind, sending them west with her message. She imagined the tiny seeds rising, drifting, lifting over the hills, over the river, down with the stream, drawing along the invisible line now stretched taut from her to her—

"Close yourself! Close! You're so wide open I could walk right in and take your mind."

A woman with hair a dusty black-brown and eyes of deep blue—the deep dark blue of the dome of sky late in summer when the day turns towards night, but dark won't fall, not quite, because summer wants to stay, hold on to the world, linger forever. Blue eyes, royal blue, endlessly deep, and Peretur, helpless, fell in. A roar in her ears, a rush, a gush and cataract of self, one into the other, poured back and forth, back and forth: a man lying on his back, face shimmering with water-light, a lake—the lake, her lake—Nimuë's lake, so—

With a snap, the way closed and Peretur was sitting on the stone, swaying, holding a bald dandelion.

The woman knelt by Peretur, close enough to touch her on the knee, though she did not. "Peretur," she said, tasting the name.

For a moment Peretur could not speak, only sit with sensation flickering up and down her belly and back, like a school of fish swimming in and out of the light. She reached out to the woman before her, slowly, with a hand that felt torn off and reattached, as though it were not hers. The woman before her was closed now, tight as a fist, but they had just lain open to one another, and she knew her. She touched the tips of the woman's hair where it curled on her collarbone.

It looked dense and soft as powdered charcoal but felt sleek as a seal. "You're Nimuë. You drowned the king's sorcerer. And I've been looking for your lake all my life."

"He's not dead," said Nimuë.

Peretur blinked, and the strange underwater image of the man lying on stone dissolved to mist. She swayed again, and this time Nimuë steadied her.

They looked at each other.

"Well," Nimuë said. They looked at each other some more. "We will speak of this, but it can wait. Soon you'll get cold and start to shake. You'll need food, something hot. But, by the lake, Peretur, you must guard yourself!"

Peretur did not argue, she did not think of arguing. They were in accord; even though she could no longer see into Nimuë, in that shared moment she felt—and knew Nimuë felt—that they had known each other all their lives. And with this meeting, a thing was set in its rightful place, seated securely, and sealed. She was not sure what, or how, but one day soon she would. Meanwhile, she felt uncertain in both her legs and her mind.

"I'll help you," Nimuë said.

And she did. She helped Peretur to her feet, and Peretur felt another help, like an unseen shield over her head, as they made their way down the path. By the time they saw the outer walls of Caer Leon, her legs were steadier, though inside she felt a shiver like an ash key twirling too fast in the wind. She reached inside to still the shiver.

"Don't," said Nimuë. "Let me. Rest. You're safe. Soon you'll be right as rain, but for now, let me."

꩜

THE HOUSEMAN WHO was tending the hearth saw Nimuë, the king's sorcerer, and Peretur, who would one day be a Companion if the hall gossip was to be believed—or perhaps killed in rage by the king; who could tell with kings?—enter the hall holding each other as though they had been struck by lightning, and ran into the kitchen in a panic. But once wiser heads took charge, when Lady Nimuë and Lord Peretur had been seated on a bench by the fire and the fire stoked high, they were informed the king was still with the queen in the bower, breaking his fast, but he would no doubt wish the lord and lady fed, if they so desired?

They did so desire. They also, the Lady said, desired a fur for the lord, and then to be left alone to discuss a matter of some import.

For some time they said nothing but *Pass the jug,* and *Give me the potted mushroom,* and they ate like wolves, but at the end of her first tankard of ale Peretur shrugged off the fur, and halfway down the second tankard, she looked at Nimuë, and waited.

"Myrddyn is not dead, though he deserves to be. We'll speak more of this later. And yes, I'm Nimuë, counsellor to Arturus king, and keeper of the lake. And you are Peretur, who has been seeking my lake all your life."

"And you. I was searching for you." For now that they sat close Peretur understood that the cool depths she had dreamt of lived as much in this woman as in the lake.

"But, Peretur Paladr Hir, I knew nothing of you. I had no idea you breathed and walked the earth until you opened the Overland as easily as a book and hurled a bright flame into the sky, bright as a beacon. Why did I not know? And how can a woman so powerful be also so foolish?"

A woman. But of course, she would know that.

"Ah, you don't even know what you did. You have thrown out a signal bright enough to draw any who can hear and see; now they will be clamouring to enter you, to know you, to have you as a bee might climb inside a flower. And like a bee they will strip you bare and leave heavy with all that makes you who you are."

The shiver inside Peretur was now still. She felt very tired. "There are such folk?"

"Perhaps not folk, not all of them."

Two housemen left the bower carrying a covered bowl and ewer, towels, and a large tray.

"Artos will soon summon me. But you'll be needing to sleep, and it's best you do. You might sleep the day away. I'll send word you're not to be disturbed. So go now, sleep, but guard yourself. And tomorrow, come to the lake. We will plumb this mystery."

PERETUR'S DREAMS WERE brightly coloured and confused. She woke late in the day—by her bed there was food and a covered jug that had not been there before—looked about, thought perhaps she should get up and go check on

Bony and Broc, but fell back into sleep before she could do anything about it. And as the afternoon darkened, so did her dreams.

It was subtle at first: an image of her mother sitting outside the cave—outside, even before the trees had leafed out!—with her eyes closed, more silver-tin threads in her hair, hands moving over her scrying bowl, saying over and over, *Bêr-hyddur, the geas is broken. Bêr-hyddur . . .*

Then overhead a blazing streak, growing, widening, thickening, like the trail left in the night sky by a burning arrow, reaching an arc, and soon to fall, down and down to its target sitting small and revealed in the clearing beside a cave.

And along the glowing gold path, following it, came another. She felt him but could not see him; he walked in mist, unseen, but he walked the bright path she had laid for him, the clear bright path to what once was hidden. Then the shape in the mist gestured, and she was pushed from her own dream, and slept deep.

An hour before dawn, another dream, though less like a dream than an echo, or a message. *Peretur, come to the lake as quick as you may. Do not stray from the path. And guard yourself!*

Guard yourself, Peretur thought when she woke up. *Bêr-hyddur,* she thought again as she dressed. *Bêr-hyddur, the geas is broken . . .*

❧

SHE TOOK THREE apples, one for Bony and one for Broc—to give when she passed the byre on the way to the gate—and one for herself as she walked. The small door, Nimuë's gate, opened to a touch, and closed itself behind her. The path was steep and winding, narrow in some places, wider in others, but never hidden. Perhaps she should have ridden. But no horse would fit through that gate, and without knowing how, she knew—nonetheless knowing it as she knew the weight of her own tread and the bend in her left little finger—that she could ride around the outer palisade and find no path but the ones to the spring, to the road, and to the village. The only way to the lake was through Nimuë's gate, and only Nimuë could grant permission.

Her apple was soon gone, and she almost threw the core aside, then wondered what such uncanny earth might do with seeds—and she tucked it instead into her cuff.

The path seemed ordinary enough; she felt grit under her boot, and dust rose and fell as it should, and the grass to either side looked and sounded like good hill grass, dotted with clover and daisies. She could not see the place where the real land blended into the magical, only that if she looked into the distance it was not the same ranks of rising green hills as she might see from near the spring. This was wilder land, with heather and gorse, and a tang in the air she could not place. And the path climbed steeply enough that she was glad she had not had to climb it yesterday. As she walked, the dirt underfoot grew thinner and she felt the bedrock near the surface; here and there it broke through in jagged grey chunks. Now she smelt juniper, and thought she glimpsed the still-mostly-white flash of a mountain hare—

like the hares that lived in the snow in winter in Ystrad Tywi. The air smelt a little thinner, too, but what drew her attention was the scent that had called her all her life: the deep, clear, cold song of the lake.

Between one breath and the next she stood on its shore.

It was a lake on the flat top of a mountain, and in its centre was an island or perhaps a great rock fallen in the Long Ago: smooth-faced around its base, but jagged and craggy and tall above. And all of it bare as an egg; no birds nested in those crags and no lichen grew in its crevices.

The sky was blue, the sun shone on the path, and there was no wind, but the lake lapped iron grey and choppy against the circular shore, and the slap of the water on rock spoke of sides that fell down straight and steep. The lake was deep, and bigger than any she had heard tell of. If the path around it were a circle, it might take two hours to walk.

She smelt woodsmoke, ordinary applewood, and followed it perhaps a third of the way around the lake, to a house. It seemed built of real log and dressed with real stone, the roof not thatched but sheathed in tile. Against the wall facing the lake was a bench, plainly but honestly made. The well was built of dressed stone, the rope wound around its iron bar strong hemp. The path to the door seemed a continuation of the path around the lake, and the door was open.

Nimuë knelt inside by the hearth, humming, leaning forward to swing a kettle over the flames. When Peretur crossed the threshold, Nimuë looked round sharply, then hissed and shook her hand.

Peretur crossed the stone flags and knelt. "Are you burnt?"

The great vein at the side of Nimuë's neck fluttered. "No. Yes. That is, you startled me and the kettle is hot. It's nothing."

"May I see?"

Nimuë held out her hand, not close enough to touch, but to see. She was right; it would not even need an onion poultice.

The onion made her think of her apple core, and she pulled it from her cuff. "Is it safe to bury this here?"

Nimuë's face closed and her blue eyes grew more blue as their centres shrank to dots. "What do you mean?"

"I . . . Just that it is soggy in my cuff."

"Why did you bring it to me today?"

Peretur did not know what she had done wrong. "I didn't bring it. That is, I brought three apples, one for each of my horses and one for me. I ate this on the walk, and thought throwing it off the path might not be wise."

Nimuë searched her face for a moment, then took a breath, and laughed—not a real laugh, but a try at a real laugh. She held her hand out for the apple core and tossed it in the fire. "I'm sorry. I'm flustered, because you startled me. No one has startled me in twenty years, Peretur Paladr Hir, not since I was a child. And now you have done it twice." She checked the flame under the kettle, and stirred the logs with a poker—though the flames seemed fine to Peretur. "Artos is afraid of you, and I begin to understand why."

The king, afraid? Of her?

"My path should have warned me of your climb. The lake

should have spoken to me of your arrival. They did not. I felt nothing, heard nothing, only the murmur, stronger than usual, of his—" She sat back on her heels, blue eyes fixed on Peretur's face.

"What—"

Nimuë waved her back, and stood. She took Peretur by the arm, led her to the open door, and tilted her face to the light. She traced Peretur's jaw, nodded. "So very like." She reached to touch Peretur's hair. "The same, though not as dark."

Peretur went very still. "You know my mother?"

"Your mother?" Nimuë looked a little unwell. "That was who you reached out to yesterday? What is her name?"

The geas is broken. She could speak if she chose, but she was not ready to choose because she did not understand. "Who am I like? What about an apple made you wary? And why is a king afraid of me?"

Nimuë looked strained.

"Unless you give me an answer, you'll have none from me."

"To answer one is to answer all."

Peretur waited.

Nimuë sighed. "Come with me."

❦

BEHIND THE OLD elm table, to one side of the hearth, was a hanging, and behind the hanging a hidden door. Beyond the door was a blank rock chamber. Nimuë closed the door and with a word passed her hand across it until all that was visible was a silvery seam. Behind her, in the floor, a second seam appeared. Another word, and the seam became a trap-door.

The steps leading down were hewn of the same grey rock as the island in the middle of the lake, and the rock, or perhaps even the air itself, lent light to their passage as they moved down, down and down in what seemed a never-ending descent, long enough for stars to be born and worlds crumble to dust. Peretur felt as though she were crossing to another Where, another When. They walked on, and on. Some endless time later, there were no more steps, and now they were in a long tunnel, and its walls were cold and breathed damp; they were under the lake.

The other end of the tunnel led to more rock stairs, leading up, which became an upward-sloping passage, and soon sand was gritting under Peretur's feet. The air filled with a susurrus of sound.

๛

FAR ABOVE, THE rock chamber was open at the top to a small circle of grey sky, grey as the lake. The chamber's white sand floor was circular, and in the centre lay a slab of brown-grey rock, rock so dense it looked slippery, like calf's liver. On it, upon a raw sheepskin, lay a man.

He lay still but his mouth moved, and he murmured, endless as the sea. His eyes were open and tracked back and forth as though he were watching something. His hair was like her mother's, dark bronze with a heavy wave, though with no tin streaks. Peretur had never seen a clean-shaven man so close before. In the watery light his chin and cheeks, even his neck, glittered here and there with flecks of gold and bronze, as though a thief, shaving coins, had, startled, thrown the curls of soft metal in his face. His eyes were grey-blue, like a new-forged blade darkening after the coals, a blade left too long unhammered, spoiling; new, but ruined.

"This is Myrddyn," Nimuë said. "If your mother's name is Elen, he is her brother."

Her mother had a brother. Myrddyn. Sorcerer, chief counsellor to Arturus king. "He is young. Younger than my mother."

"No. He's older. And now he is bound, stopped forever while the rest of us age."

Myrddyn. Her mother's brother. Family. "Who did this?"

Nimuë lifted her chin. "I did."

⁖⁘⁖

THE LAKE LIVED in its own time as well as its own place. Peretur thought it should at least be late afternoon, but back at the elm table by the hearth in the cottage, the light told another story; it was barely midday.

They sat opposite each other, like enemies at truce.

"I have answered two of your questions. Now answer mine: Who did you reach out to yesterday?"

"My mother. Elen." *The geas is broken.*

"Is she still mortal?"

Mortal? Peretur had never thought about it. Elen had magics, like Nimuë, but she aged, she wept, she grew thin. Peretur nodded.

"Where is she?"

"Hidden."

"Not anymore. Tell me."

Peretur thought of the mist following the bright arrow's path. *The geas is broken.* And she was the one who broke it.

"You tell me first, why is Arturus afraid of me?"

"Because Myrddyn warned him that one day a man who was not a man might come to take his sword."

The king did not know she was not a man. "It is more than that. It's the sword."

"Yes. I've seen the way he touches it when he says your name."

"So, what is the sword? It is Myrddyn's doing, but why? And why did you bind him?"

"For that, I must tell you a story."

And though her body did not move, Nimuë seemed to distance herself, and began to speak as though of someone else.

Twelve years ago, Myrddyn, following rumours of a witch who spoke to water, found an orphaned girl on the cusp of womanhood, a girl singing and steering springs and streams to water a farmer's field, or fill a village's well, just to eat and sleep out of the rain. He praised her, and told her she could do more, so very much more, if only she would let him show her how.

And at first, he did show her. He touched his hand to her temple and entered her mind and showed her how to breathe like this, how to focus on that, and soon she could bend a river and raise a wall; she could heal a broken bone and help a tree flower. *More,* she said. *Show me more.* And so he did, though only a little at a time, and after each lesson she was strangely tired. And it was not for five years that she began to suspect that he was not teaching her, but learning alongside her, drawing from her. This was after he brought her to Arturus, who was not yet king. To Arturus and his men, who were not yet Companions of the king, she was Myrddyn's pretty pupil, kneeling at her master's feet. And always, in private, he urged her on in the great search, the search of searches: for a treasure, a thing of power. Urging became demanding; he would lay his palm on her cheek and inside her mind drive her on, on, always on.

The day came when the girl was standing in a stream bed, listening to the river, persuading it to flow a little more this way, and he was standing on the bank—how he hated to get wet! Just like a cat—and he told her to stop, there was something more important he needed from her just now. But she was feeling strong, feeling good, and she said, *No, this won't take long.* And was shocked by a wave of rage, his thoughts of what he would do to the annoying, ungrateful little bitch when he didn't need her anymore. She stopped, stock-still with shock, there in midstream, and stared at him. But he did not know anything was amiss, he didn't feel it. He was smiling a false smile, saying with his voice, *Very well. Just this once, pretty bird, have your way.* But his heart spoke another story; she could read him like a fish split and spread on a bake stone, and inside he stank of the urge to power—

Nimuë stopped. "He couldn't get inside me—had never been able to—without touch. But there I was, strides away, reading him. I knew then that I was more powerful than him. Greater. He'd been . . ." By the set of her face the next words were hard. "In the guise of helping me he had been . . . drinking me."

Sipped and drained like a wine cup. Peretur almost reached across the table, but Nimuë had gone away inside again.

—Myrddyn was all the girl knew. He was her only friend, her only family, her teacher. And so for a little while she said nothing, did nothing—but as they looked for the treasure, she looked into him, reaching deeper and deeper . . .

With a visible wrench Nimuë forced herself to be present.

"But I didn't want to stop the search. For we were seeking two of the treasures of the Tuath Dé—"

Peretur blinked. "The Tuath Dé are real?"

"The stone is real. As you see. We found it—I found it, when I found my way to the lake—and through me, so did Myrddyn. If only I'd known then what I know now. But I didn't know. Believe me, Peretur, I didn't know."

Her hands were clenching and unclenching on the table. They were small compared to Peretur's but not soft, not weak. Good hands.

"So, we found the stone, and with it the sword—which the stone hid, as it now hides Myrddyn."

"Arturus's sword."

"Myrddyn led him to it; Artos claimed it and became king. It's how he remains king. Whoever holds the sword will not be defeated in battle. Whoever holds the sword holds some part of its power. Artos recognises you, Peretur. Perhaps he sees the resemblance to Myrddyn. But perhaps it's more, Myrddyn's warning: someone coming for the sword, coming to take his power. And the sword itself recognises you. Why?"

Nimuë was closing herself off, ready to push her away. "Nimuë . . ."

"Why?"

"It . . . draws me."

"You look so like him." Her hands clenched, unclenched. "But you don't feel like him." She took a deep breath, put her shoulders back, and spoke in a deep, formal voice. "Peretur Paladr Hir, do you, like Myrddyn, seek the power of the Tuath Dé?"

"I thought they were a story." The Tuath Dé. The four treasures. Were they all real, all the stories her mother told her? Nimuë was waiting. "I didn't even know the sword was here."

"Yet now you do. So, I will ask once again: Will you take it?"

"No!" Nimuë flinched. "No. I won't take the sword. I don't want it." Peretur felt very tired. The sword both drew her and repelled her. It was not for her, she knew this though she did not know how she knew it. She could not tell if Nimuë believed her. "Why do we fight over this? I don't want the sword. I have never wanted the sword. They are malicious gods, these Tuath, to make such things to fight over."

"Gods? What is a god? These treasures are all that remains to the Tuath of the power of their homeland. What power do they have of their own? I don't know. They fight for these treasures. The Tuath were never many, but now when they lose a treasure, they diminish. Any who may be left have, still, great power lent by the treasures. But when we have hidden all the treasures I believe that power will fade. They will fade from the land, fade from memory, and be gone."

"You want them gone?"

"I want their treasures gone, where no mortal can find them ever again. When mortals use that power, they are terrible. But to understand that, you need to hear the rest of the story. Will you hear it?"

"I will hear it."

"Artos took and held the sword, and, through him, Myrddyn began to draw on the power of the Tuath. But that power is not meant for human hands. Even Artos, who has no magic to be corrupted, will pay for it—he does already; the sword eats at his mind. For Myrddyn, a sorcerer open to its power, who used it to grow younger—as I think he once used your mother, as you will see—it began to drive him mad with want."

Nimuë looked down at the grain in the elm table. Peretur wished she could read her.

Nimuë sighed and looked up. "No. That's only what is more comfortable for me to believe. It did not begin with the sword. Myrddyn was mad, I think, long before we met. I should have seen, but I didn't. Or perhaps I did but I didn't want to know—until that day when I looked deep inside him, and could not unsee what was so plain."

She folded her hands together on the table, lifted her chin, and looked straight at Peretur.

"I'm afraid."

"Of me?"

"Of what you will think of me. And, yes, perhaps of you, too, a little."

"Why?"

"The Tuath can speak to the things of power, and the power can speak in them. They are not gods, but neither are they mortal. The sword speaks to you, and speaks of you, as it never could to Myrddyn, or me, or Artos. The sword was not made by mortals for mortals. And it speaks to you. And you smell of its makers. So the question now, Peretur, is: Are you wholly mortal?"

She did not know.

"And now we're at the point where words are not enough. I'm human, I can't help but shade the truth to feel better about myself. For the bare, plain truth we must let each other in, as we did before. But that was brief, a moment, just a touch. This would be . . . more. And I'm afraid. It is an . . . unclean thing to have another more powerful inside you."

Unclean. "You think I'm unclean?" Unclean, while to her Nimuë felt like the lake: cool, wide, deep. Her voice shook. "Did you find me unclean when I was open to you?"

"Inside you is like a forest I have never seen before, with a path that I know goes deep, deep into the unknown. What if I follow that path and at its end find you are like Myrddyn?"

Peretur wanted to trust this woman, trust her own judgement, but twice before she had trusted that she had won herself a place, and twice misjudged. *Unclean* . . . She felt herself tearing slowly down the middle. "I could have lost myself in you. I was willing." Part of her still was. She stood up. "I must go."

"From Caer Leon?"

Leave. Run away again. Was that what she wanted? To be driven away, again? "Just from here, from the lake, from you." She turned to the door, then turned back. "It was not an unclean thing!"

Nimuë looked tired and sad. "This is not finished."

☙❦❧

THE SUN WAS still shining when she came down the path and closed Nimuë's gate behind her. Despite the sunlight, Caer Leon seemed small and drab, dreary with rough wood and bare dirt. In the byre, Bony and Broc seemed surprised to see her again so soon, and she remembered, again, that time was different by the lake. She patted them, and promised them a ride and a treat later.

In the outer practice yard, on the other side of the inner fort, she heard the clash of weapons, the occasional shout and hoot of laughter. The Companions were training, half on foot, half on horse.

She leaned against the rough wood palisade by the practice spears, arms folded, and watched. How slow they seemed, how foolish in their fine leathers.

"Ho, Pretty Per!" Cei, pulling off his helm. He nodded for his sparring partner to continue with the exercise, and walked over. "Where've you been? No point going off sulking just because Artos is in one of his moods. He'll come around. Meanwhile, the Eingl are massing and I need to see how you fight with others. Go get your sword."

She looked at him, standing with his muscled legs wide,

fair hair stuck to his head, in his tawdry green-and-yellow leathers and suddenly, very much, wanted to hit something. Cei would do.

She pushed herself off the wall, took one of the spears with blunted tips and twirled it in her hands. "I don't need a sword," she said.

Cei studied her. Then he turned and shouted over his shoulder at a compact, brown-haired man, "Llywarch! Let's see how fast our new formation can take down this insolent puppy."

A few of the Companions on foot stopped to watch. Llywarch beckoned and two of his men, one right-handed, the other left-handed, overlapped their round shields, with Llywarch at the centre holding a pike two-handed, pointing between the shields, and the other two with swords at either side.

"I call it the point," Cei said. "It's designed to—"

Peretur knocked them down in three fast sweeps: low to the legs of the man on the left of the point, or her right; when he fell, a whirl and turn and thump on the back of Llywarch's head; then a vicious stop-thrust against the other's shield which sent him staggering back at such speed his legs could not keep up and he tangled in the fallen pike and went down. She twirled her spear and smiled, a hard flex of muscle and bone. She would take them all, one at a time, and she would not be gentle.

One of the horsemen kneed his black forward, reached down a hand, and hauled the right-handed man to his feet. Llanza. No one said anything, but Peretur remembered these were not enemies but Companions. She gave a hand to the first man, which after a moment he took. He pulled himself up, then had to hop to the bench by the wall. Cei looked down at Llywarch, who was sitting up trying to get his helm off. "Looks like it'll need Afan to get that off." Llywarch didn't seem to hear him. Cei pointed to two men, then Llywarch, then the armoury, then turned back to Peretur.

"Your point doesn't work," she said.

"Not against a lunatic with a spear," he said. "Go get your sword."

"The sword is not my weapon."

"Listen, petal cheeks. The Eingl fight in shield walls, on foot. A horse won't charge that, and lone champions get killed. In the Companions, there are no lone champions; we fight together. We follow orders. If I say get your sword, you get your sword. Do you want to be a Companion?"

To fight together. To belong. "I'll get my sword."

Cei was disgusted when he found her sword still lacked a tip, so he brought two from the armoury: one short, for stabbing, one longer, like Talorcan's. She started with the short sword, taking the right-hand position in a point, with egg-shaped Geraint on the pike and Cei himself taking the left. Six men armed with shields, spears, and stabbing knives opposed them.

She had never worked with others before. At first she did not understand that she should not take any opening that offered itself—no easy strike to a man with a careless gap between chin and shield rim—but stay, always, in the formation until told. She found it difficult to move at their

97

strange, heavy pace, hard to keep her left shoulder down and in against Geraint, and her right shoulder always turned away a little to give room for her sword against any who attacked from the side. But the first time their shields interleaved, and they stepped forward together at Cei's barked command, she felt a strange flicker, a doubling of self that was part Cei's strength, part Geraint's steadiness—but then they lost their stride and it was just her on one side and Cei on the other, with Geraint holding the long heavy pike in the middle. Then as the six men opposite advanced, Cei called, "Tighter!" and the point's shields interlocked and held, and then she did not feel Cei, she did not feel Geraint, she did not feel her own boots on the ground; she felt a sliding meld into a third thing that moved with shared purpose. She shivered, as she had the first time she had watched dawn over the duck pond while a blackbird sang. For one brief moment the three of them were one, and they stood against the six attackers almost without effort. They knocked them down—one, two-three-four, five-six—and then it was just the three of them.

Peretur laughed aloud, delighted. "Is it always like that?"

Geraint put the butt of the pike in the dirt and unlaced the chin of his helmet. "It is never like that."

Cei, for once, was lost for words. Then he blinked. "Again. But this time I watch."

He put her with other groups; he had her be one of the attackers. He had her try left side, and once with point. Once or twice in other groups, either on the left or the right, she felt a momentary flicker of that shared purpose, and she thought Andros might have, too—he gave her a thoughtful look—but it was not until she worked again with Geraint, this time with Beli on the left, that it flared again, stronger than before, and for longer.

"Good," said Cei. "Oh, very good. You two"—to Geraint and Beli—"go work with others and help them find it. You"—to Peretur. "Let's see how those strawberry cheeks look on a horse. I tell you, if you're even half as good in the saddle as on foot, Artos would be mad to refuse you."

And while a boy was sent to fetch Broc, she watched the points practicing. It seemed to her that those she had worked with before seemed to do better than the others.

A horse whuffed on her shoulder: Llanza's black. "This thing you have done." He was watching the men. "Is it to be trusted?"

Peretur did not know how to answer.

Then Broc was being led across the yard, coat gleaming and neck arched, lifting his hooves high. He danced a little as the boy handed Peretur the reins. "Eager, are you?" She stroked his neck, felt the muscles bursting with life. He was eager, more than eager, and so was she. She swung into the saddle.

Llanza called to Cei, "Weapons?"

"Sword and spear. Held, not thrown. Try not to kill the boy. But test him."

One on one like champions of old? She called for the second sword, the longer one. *Oh, my lovely,* she told Broc as she settled the tip of its scabbard behind her, drew the blade partway, and slammed it home, *Oh, now we will show them a thing or two.*

"Well, Prietu," Llanza said, patting his black. "Are you ready?" Then to Peretur, "Over there, where there's room." And he cantered away. She watched him. She had never seen a man so easy in the saddle; it was his element, like water for a fish. Indeed, as she watched, he looped the reins around the pommel of his saddle, where he had affixed a kind of horn, and—with no more thought than a man sitting before his own fire—leaned one way for his lance, to settle under his arm, and the other for his shield, and at the same time brought Prietu in a smooth curve and stopped dead, with no word, and no other communication than his body.

"Show-off," she shouted, and even she could hear the eagerness in her voice. Then she thought: *I have forgotten my gauntlets.* But Llanza wasn't wearing them, either, and though both spears as they were lowered into position gleamed sharp, both were armed only in scaled leather shirts and helms.

He was sizing her up, too. Broc was taller, Llanza's spear a little longer.

There seemed to be no moment of beginning, they were simply thundering at each other. Both aimed true, both shifted their shields at the right time and right angle and deflected the sharp tips away. Again, they both brought their mounts around in a smooth tight curve, and without pause were moving straight for each other.

As they came together again, a divot of dirt flicked from

the black's hoof to Broc's chest, and Peretur felt, a hair of a moment before he moved, Llanza rise in his stirrups and thrust the spear forward and to the side, and she swayed, boneless as a twist of cloth as Broc swerved. The spear missed and she felt a ripple of surprise run through the men in the yard.

"Ha!" Broc's heart beat huge and strong in his chest, and this was a worthy adversary.

This time when they came together they both split and parted at the same moment, and Peretur warned Broc, so he was braced, then leaned and reached out, far out, far to her left, and far back, and banged her shield on Llanza's so that, for a moment, he swayed over his pommel before Prietu was under him again.

And now he grinned, and she felt him adjust, felt the black change his gait as his rider girded himself for real effort.

They would write songs of what followed: the horses dancing; the spears flickering like swords, faster than the eye could see; Llanza's perfect seat; Peretur's grace, lithe as a cat; the sweat running down their mounts' flanks. The crack of Llanza's spear as it split.

"Swords!" shouted Cei.

Peretur flung away the boar spear and hauled out her sword, and part of her was aware of excitement from the yard, shouts here and there.

"Away shields!"

They both threw them aside. And as though being free of the weight freed some other part of her, she flowed from one state to another, and now instead of a solid object moving to or from a target, she became liquid, pouring to and around it. And now she could read Llanza's horse as easily as her own; she could read his intent as simple as breathing.

And still he kept up with her. She moved faster, and so did he. She leaned farther, and so did he. Then she began to draw on the life around her—the hum in the air, the flight of the kicked dirt—and changed again. Now she felt she could move anywhere, any way, effortless as wind or mist. She could overwhelm him, cover him, smother him as—

—as an immortal would a mortal. *Unclean.*

She faltered, and Broc wrong-footed, and Llanza slammed into her and the sword fell from her hand.

She clutched her saddle, swaying, and stared at the sword in the dirt. There was great noise, and Broc's ribs heaved between her legs. He hung his head, working for air. She had driven him too hard. Was this what Nimuë was afraid of? Was it her true nature to take from others for her own power?

Then she and Llanza were surrounded by men shouting themselves hoarse, shouting and cheering, and she saw that after their hard focus the abrupt change had shocked Llanza almost as much as her.

He pulled off his helm, swung his leg up and over Prietu, and slid off the horse's back in a way she knew she would never match, even if she lived the rest of her life in the saddle. She fumbled off her own helm and dismounted respectably, reassured herself with a pat that Broc was well—already lifting his head, immensely pleased with himself—and when Llanza held out his arm, they clasped each other's forearm, and leaned in. They rested forehead to forehead for a moment, then Llanza slapped her on the shoulder. Men whistled. He grinned. "For one who has no whiskers yet, you fight like the Reaper of Arawn!"

Arawn. Not mortal.

He turned to the other men. "Peretur Paladr Hir would have had me if his horse hadn't stumbled. I'm proud to name him brother!" Then from the side of his mouth, "Smile, brother. Today you are a champion."

Peretur made herself grin, and shouted over the hubbub, "You're unfair to my horse, Lord Llanza! He did nothing wrong. The fault was all mine."

Broc preened. Prietu arched his neck. "Then let us take care of your faultless mount and mine."

It was the best and easiest way to get rid of their audience. Llanza sent a houseboy to fetch food and ale to the byre.

In the byre they worked in silence for a while, until Prietu and Broc were cooled down, rubbed dry, combed out, and settled in their stalls.

Llanza collapsed onto a stool by the tray of food while Peretur checked Bony's hay net and stroked his nose. "Come, sit. You must be exhausted."

She was not. Pleasantly used, but not even really tired. She could not tell him that. There were so many things she could tell no one. *Are you wholly mortal?*

"You're doing it again," Llanza said. "You get the look of a man haunted by guilt. Anyone might believe you're keeping a dreadful secret. Well, there is no secret I know of that can't be helped by food. So for pity's sake come sit, and while we eat we'll talk of what's to be done about Artos."

That soft note again. She heard the secret, perhaps a secret no one wholly mortal should hear. It was hard to tell what she was and was not supposed to know or do. Was this, too, unclean?

She settled down on a pile of straw, took a hand pasty, and bit into it. She closed her eyes, trying to tell what she was eating. Tarragon. Vinegar. And . . .

"Coney," Llanza said. "I showed the cook how we do it in Astur. Gwen is greedy for them."

She opened her eyes and took another bite, let the food distract her from what she was not supposed to know.

"You too, I see." Llanza smiled. "You look like the priests at Mass who pretend they have seen a vision of the Christ."

She chewed and swallowed. She eyed her pasty, torn between hunger and curiosity. "Who is this Christ?"

"Don't ask me. While many in my country are what the local priest would call heretics, I'm not even that. Bedwyr's the one who wears the cross, ask him."

She sighed, put down her pasty, and started to stand.

"Not right now! Eat, eat. I'll answer as best I can."

Christ is a god, he said. Or perhaps the son of a god—people seemed to disagree unhappily about that. He was born on Earth, but then died, but then woke up again, and then died again—or perhaps didn't die, that part was a confusion to him. By all accounts Christ lived in heaven, surrounded by angels and his father, and some sort of other brother god, or spirit—a ghost. Also in heaven were an assortment of men and women, who though born mortal, became immortal, or what the Christers called saints. And if you sent them messages—

"How do you send messages?"

"It's called praying. You just . . . ask in your head."

Perhaps she was a saint. "And do they answer?"

"The holiest say they have dreams, or visions, and that is their god talking. And it's these holy men and women who, when they die, become saints. Though how we know someone is a saint I don't know; ask Bedwyr. But men build Christ temples, churches, in their name—we have one here, for Saint Cadog. Men build the churches and go there to pray, to ask a saint, like Cadog, to intercede with the Christ—or maybe his father, I don't really understand that part. But they ask the saint to ask the Christ for something."

"What sort of thing?"

"A new horse, a cure for a sick child. They ask for what matters most. So you, Peretur, you might perhaps ask that the king make you a Companion."

Peretur finished her pasty and picked up another.

"Bedwyr might tell you, *If you want the king to change his mind, go ask Cadog's priest to petition for you.* Certainly that's what he told me to tell you."

Her heart kicked; Bony nickered. "You have talked to people about me? To Bedwyr?"

"Say rather that he has talked to me. As has Andros. And Beli. And Geraint. And Cei. All of them. Even before today. They saw you fight Cei. If they did not understand Artos's refusal then, it will be worse now. And you know what Cei's like, a badger who won't let go of a thing once he has his jaws around it. His advice to you would not be Bedwyr's."

He snorted. "Cei is more likely to tell you the priest is a sot, no use to man or beast, and your best bet would be to go shout at the king, and get all your friends to shout at the king, until the poor man so yearns for peace he gives in."

"Would that work?"

"Cei has already shouted at the king. Artos was not pleased."

They, too, thought she belonged here, as one of them. "And you? What would you advise?"

"I would not advise but ask: Are you sure? Artos does not often change his mind. You must be sure, because it will be a hard road. You must be very clear that this is what you want. And you must know why you want it."

"I am sure. It is what I want. I belong here. I dreamt of this place as a child. Caer Leon and the people in it are like no one and nowhere else. It feels . . . clean. Being here is like standing at the edge of the sea under a wide sky: clear, open, clean, and bright. Here is where I am meant to be."

"Must it be as a Companion?"

"I want to fight among you. The Companions fight for what is good and true and clean." She cast about for something he might understand. "You fight not to take or break but to make."

"We fight for Artos, for his vision. He sees the isle as one kingdom; he wants to return it to how it was before the Redcrests left, with one law for all to follow, good roads, and much besides. Though sometimes I'm not sure Cei always sees it that way. He would not have pardoned defeated men and left them free to become bandits. Trouble will come of it, he told Artos. He was right."

"But so was the king. Most of those who became bandits were good, decent folk; they would farm if they could. He is right to try. Right to hope for it, right to fight for it. That's what I would fight for."

"To hear you talk is like hearing him talk when he first became king." He seemed troubled.

"And now?"

"He worries. He needs an heir, someone to pass the flame to, to keep the dream alive. The longer he must wait, the more he worries. He fondles his sword and he worries about who will wield it after him. He—" Llanza sighed. "I am tired, Peretur Paladr Hir. I should not have said that."

"The sword is important to him."

"I wish he had never found it. It seems to prey on his mind. And when I talked to him and Gwen about you, he gripped it and said, *He's come for the sword. Myrddyn warned me.* I wish, too, Myrddyn had never found us. Sorcerers have no place in Caer Leon."

No mention of the sorcerer's message of a man who is not a man. Perhaps Llanza did not know that part of the warning. Perhaps she should tell him; she was so tired of wondering who knew what. But that was not her secret to share. "Then I'm glad he's gone."

"Aye. And though Nimuë's another of his kind, Gwen trusts her. When Artos won't listen to reason, he'll listen to Gwen, who listens to Nimuë."

"And to you."

He nodded, and rubbed his face as he had the first time she had seen him, after the fight in the valley. "Peretur, I don't know what's got into me, talking of such things. It seems I trust you. Gwen wants to trust you. But there's something—we all feel it. And we know nothing of you. You appear from nowhere, save our lives, then disappear. Then reappear on a horse, moving like the very air itself. I've never in my life seen anyone move like that. Who taught you to ride?"

"My horse."

"No. Truly."

"Truly. I learnt from my horse. I had no one else."

"Not your father?"

"I never knew my father."

"Ah. So that's the way of it. A boy needs a father, as I know to my cost." He shook himself. "But that is a tale for another time. So. Now. You, Peretur, a champion among men, have no father, and a mother who grows peas. This does not sound so terrible a secret. Do you worry people will laugh?"

"Cei does laugh."

"Cei laughs at everyone but his king. He holds you in high esteem. No, the best thing to do with a fear is to face it. Will you not tell Artos who you are?"

She laughed in bitter amusement. She did not know who she was. And it would make no difference. "The king has set his mind against me, and no amount of words will change it. And it—it's so unfair! This is where I'm meant to be—*who* I'm meant to be!"

Broc neighed, a shattering sound in the small byre, and Bony kicked the wall of his stall.

I am afraid, Nimuë had said. Yes, and so was she; even the horses knew it. But *the best thing to do with a fear is face it.*

⟐

AGAIN THEY SAT at the elm table.

"Are you still afraid?" Peretur said.

"I am."

"Two days ago, what I felt . . ." Nimuë, cool and deep and clear as the lake. "I can't believe it is unclean."

"That was not."

"But—"

"But when unwilling, it is. I have seen it."

"With Myrddyn?"

Nimuë hesitated, then nodded. "But beyond that. With others. And worse."

Peretur wanted to reach out and touch her hand, but Nimuë looked brittle enough to fly apart. So she just waited.

"The worse . . . The worse is about you—no, not because of you; you're not worse. But it is close to you. And to explain it, for you to know it, you'll have to feel it through me. And I will have to feel you feel it. I'm afraid, yes, but I will do this thing, if you're willing."

⟐

THIS TIME THEY did not fall into each other unprepared; they held each other by both wrists, and breathed, and entered together. It made no difference. It was like riding a vast cataract, tumbling and falling, flying past life laid out like a story on the riverbanks—Nimuë falling into Myrddyn, seeing his weakness; Peretur stealing a hatchet. Then back further—Peretur tracing the figures engraved on the bowl; Nimuë bending the path of a raindrop trickling down her own arm. Then faster, and further, and back and forth, a maelstrom of sound and scent and feeling. Memories of their own and memories they had from others, who in turn had them from yet others, all jumbled together—animals and plants, clouds and riverbanks, breasts and mouths, battles and terrors. Everything. All of it.

Yet because Nimuë was showing her, it was also distinct, orderly, like a forest floor after a storm that, if you stepped back and looked from a distance, you could read for what fell from where, and when.

Myrddyn was born far to the north, north even of Gwynedd, in Elmet. As a small boy he began practicing magics—to look inside the frogs he caught, to see how their hearts beat and stilled at a touch, then the foxes he trapped as he grew older—and was fourteen when his sister, Elen, was born and their mother died. Elen was stronger in magic than Myrddyn, and, like her brother, silver-witted and proud. Myrddyn was as a mother and father to her; she followed him without question. They were better, stronger, more comely than everyone they knew, he told her: they would be as gods.

Elen as a very small girl began to sense the presence of the Tuath who walked the Overland. With Myrddyn she spied on them squabbling over their treasures. Two treasures, the sword and the stone, were already stolen, and lost, then found, and lost again, each time weakening the Tuath. And Myrddyn hatched a plan: when next the Tuath fought over a treasure, while they were weak and at war, he and Elen would steal the treasure for themselves.

And so it was that when Manandán, son of the sea, stole the greatest treasure, the cup, and, calling himself Manawydan fab Llŷr, fled over the sea from Eiru to Dyfed, he found Elen waiting. He found her beautiful—and she, being a mortal, could not help but find Manandán beautiful also, because he willed it.

Manandán and others of the Tuath had been as gods for so long they thought mortals less worthy of care and attention than raindrops. Manandán used Elen as he wanted, and she was helpless to give him back anything but devotion, even as he rived her mind and spirit, and tormented her by showing her the wicked heart of her brother—who did not love her but planned to steal the cup for himself and become as a god. And Elen, whose mind was now unmoored and swollen with repeated use, smiled and smiled—while deep, deep in the tiny corner she had held safe for herself, her rage grew.

The day Myrddyn came to steal the cup, she was ready. As her brother and her lover faced each other, Elen, for a moment, just a moment, used desperate strength to ally the cup's power to her own, and fled.

Without the treasure, Manandán was greatly weakened, and Myrddyn—still linked to Elen's strength, though not her thoughts—escaped. After some time had passed, and Myrddyn had not found his sister, or the cup, or any rumour of them—for such power was beyond him on his own—he began to seek another child to mould as he had moulded his sister, only this time he would control them from the beginning. He broke many young folk, and threw them away; he searched for years. When Peretur was seven—though he did not know Peretur existed, just as Manandán did not know—when she was eating and drinking daily from the great cup of the Tuath Dé and tracing its figures with her fingers, Myrddyn found Nimuë, and set about bending her into his tool without breaking her, for although the greatest treasure, the cup, was lost to him, somehow hidden, there were others—the two he knew of whose keepers and thieves had each killed the other, taking with them their hiding place. He was not strong enough to find them on his own.

And so between them Nimuë and Myrddyn found the stone and the sword, and one day she looked deep into him and saw all he had done, and would do with the power of the treasures of the Tuath. Then she ground the seeds from a bushel of apples and added the grounds to his honey. When he fell in a swoon she used her own power to seize his mind, and with the power of the stone she both bound him and hid him from any who might look. She told Arturus that Myrddyn had gone on a quest, and watched while the king mourned a man who had used him as a puppet.

Then she guarded herself in case Manandán one day came looking for Myrddyn and the cup, or other Tuath came for the sword and the stone. And she stayed to make sure that when Arturus no longer had need of his sword she could bind it and hide it from mortal hands with the power of the stone. No mortal should taste the treasures of the Tuath, for that power would drive them to corruption and madness even as it set them as rulers over all the world.

⊙∽⊙

SHADOWS WERE GROWING long as Peretur and Nimuë faced each other across the table, hands still laced around each other's wrists.

"I was so lonely," Peretur said.

"I'm sorry. I would have come for you, if I'd known of you."

You should have known, Peretur thought. *I knew of your lake.*

But how could a mortal, even one as powerful as Nimuë, break a geas even Manandán had not breached in all his years of searching? A geas her mother had not thought twice about binding her with. But to her mother she was not a person in her own right, not Peretur Paladr Hir; she was Tâl, the payment her mother felt owed; she was Dawnged, her treasure and gift, stolen from Manandán without his knowledge. Always something owed and owned rather than loved. No one had come to find the nameless girl alone with a woman whose mind and heart were no longer whole but a handful of broken pieces. A woman who was so hurt and so afraid of being found that to protect herself she had taken away her daughter's own memory of home and of the only love she had ever had, if it was ever love.

She let go of Nimuë and sat staring at her own hands, her not-mortal hands, while Nimuë got up and cut bread and stirred soup. The world felt wide and fragile and new as though she had lately risen from her sickbed.

Her mother, Elen, was mortal. Her father, Manandán—or as he called himself here, Manawydan fab Llŷr—was not. Peretur had eaten and drunk every day from the cup of the Tuath, the cup that was said to heal any mortal of their hurts. But the power of the Tuath would turn any mortal mad; witness her mother. And the power slowly corrupted men. But Peretur was not wholly mortal. Was she mad? Was she corrupt?

"You are not mad. You are not corrupt," Nimuë said, for they were still lightly joined.

Peretur did not know if she could shut her out.

"You can. I can show you, but, if you're willing, I think we should eat first. Though the choice is yours."

A choice with so much woven into it, so many consequences, so many futures . . .

"You need food." Nimuë put the wheat bread and crock of butter on the table—Peretur's mouth flooded at the smell—and returned to the soup kettle.

The bowl of soup Nimuë put before her smelled of barley and beans and lamb. Ordinary, worldly scents. She wrapped her hands around the wooden bowl. This was real. This was the stuff of life.

They ate the soup, and bread spread with butter—when she tasted it Peretur knew the name of the cow the milk came from, and how the maid at the dairy who milked her that day had hurt her ankle from slipping on a cowpat—and because they were joined Nimuë laughed aloud. And because they were joined, Peretur laughed, too. And then she laughed because it was good to be in a world where maids milked cows, air was just air, and time moved in orderly ways. While they ate the soup made of honest broth and good herbs, they talked of this and that—how both Myrddyn and Elen had the habit of pursing their lips when they were thinking; the birds that sang in the spring of their homelands—but when the bowls were empty and the butter crock put back to cool, they fell silent. Outside, the light began to fade.

Nimuë lit a spill from the hearth, then paused, shielding the light with her hand. "Will you stay?"

Another choice with so many paths . . .

Nimuë began to light the tallow dips.

"Could you not just . . ." Peretur waved her hand.

Nimuë looked at her, then passed her hand over the dip she had lit, and it went out, and the other dips went out, and the hearth faded to black.

"I can't see," Peretur said.

"You can."

And she could. The world was different in the dark. Colours faded. Living things glowed reddish gold—there was a mouse in the pantry. Dead things once living—the table, the wool hanging—gleamed like darkened bronze. Stone glimmered silver, and iron dull zinc. She lifted her hand, looked at the skin like burnished gold, then, with a kind of twist, inside the skin, then deeper inside the bone, then deeper still—

"Come back, now. Come back." Nimuë lit the dips again, and the hearth glowed as it should. "Light is a comfort, a human thing, and it pleases me. It reminds me I'm mortal."

"But I am not."

Nimuë reached for her hand. "You are half mortal. You feel what mortals feel, you like what mortals like. You hunger, you thirst."

Her hand felt good in Peretur's, warm, more than warm.

In the flickering ochre-and-gold light, Peretur saw the heat rise in Nimuë's cheeks, and her lips redden, and her own belly warmed, and she filled with another hunger. She lifted her hand and laid it on Nimuë's upper arm, and stroked, gently.

Nimuë's breath quickened, and she in turn laid her hand on Peretur's arm. Peretur's breath sharpened, and her breasts. They looked at each other. Peretur leaned forward, just a little, and Nimuë also, and now they could smell each other, and Peretur breathed deep. She rubbed her cheek on Nimuë's and smelt butter, and salt, and smoke, and, beneath, sharp woman scent.

She knew that scent, and her need rose like the tide. She groaned and dragged her mouth down that soft, soft cheek, and Nimuë turned, and they kissed, deep and clean and strong. She stroked the side of Nimuë's breast, and Nimuë's hand was on her waist, on her belly, between her legs, and then Nimuë was holding her upright on the stool—or she would have fallen, would have slid helpless to the floor—as Nimuë found her way beneath her clothes and began to touch, delicate, teasing, taunting, until Peretur was lost to anything, to all but that hand. Then Nimuë was pulling off her dress, pushing down Peretur's breeches, pushing her down by the hearth, pushing up against her, sliding in light and heat.

Later, Peretur leaned up on her elbow and said, "Do you have a bed?"

Nimuë laughed, a rich, rippling laugh. "No, I hang from the roof like a bat, as all good sorcerers do!" Peretur laughed, too. "I have two beds."

"Two?"

"From time to time I invite visitors. Lance comes. Most often with Gwenhwyfar."

Most often?

"Once with Artos. Though those two usually go hunting together for a few days."

"Ah."

"Yes. And that knowledge would cost your life if you revealed it."

Peretur was no longer listening. She was watching the play of shadow on Nimuë's throat, and then began to kiss it, and Nimuë made a sound, and soon they were lost again.

Later, as the fire dimmed, they found Nimuë's own bed, and slept.

᠗᠗᠗

AGAIN, THE GOLD path, and the mist moving along it, scenting, questing, and Peretur called out, *Mother! Mother!* And the mist swirled and darkened, and reached out. *No,* she thought. *No! You cannot have—*

"Peretur. Peretur, love. Peretur!" Nimuë, stroking her forehead. "What is it? I felt—" She sat up. "Tell me."

"Nothing. A dream."

"It was more than a dream." Nimuë shivered and pulled the coverlet up over her shoulders.

"You're cold. We can talk about it in the morning."

"It is almost morning." Nimuë tilted her head, studying Peretur. "We need to talk about this now, I think, before you sleep again."

⚬⚬⚬

IT TOOK SOME time to stir the embers, and while the milk warmed, they dressed. Although Nimuë was plainly worried, every time one of them fastened a tie, or pulled up hose, the other remembered untying it or pulling them down, but Nimuë tapped Peretur's hand away as she tried to slide it beneath her overdress. "The milk will burn."

Spiced, buttered milk drunk halfway down, then oats added, and eaten with a spoon, and then the sky was turning pale grey.

"Now. Tell me your dream."

"It's nothing." She could not bring herself to speak of it, even to shape the words. And when she tried to think about it, it slid away slippery as a fish.

"You've had it before?"

She shrugged helplessly. The words would not come.

"You can't speak of it?"

Nod.

"This is a geas. Your mother?"

"No," Peretur managed. *Bêr-hyddur, the geas is broken.* "Not anymore." She was sweating, and now she could not even remember what she couldn't say.

118

"You broke her geas?" She sat back. "You broke a geas made with the strength of the cup? Well. I only wish you'd asked her questions."

"She wouldn't have answered."

"She would. It's the nature of a geas that when it breaks, the caster and the caught must, for a while, speak only truth."

"How long a while?"

"Perhaps we'll find out. For we must break this new geas."

They tried. They tried deep trance. They tried a spell-song Nimuë had learnt from an old village woman in the north. Peretur opened her mind and Nimuë tried to chase the memory down, twisting and turning like a sight hound coursing after a hare, but it would not be caught. They even tried a foul brew, bitter as burdock, that did nothing but purge Peretur's bowels.

By midmorning she had stopped heaving and groaning enough to manage oatmeal in plain water. While Nimuë read the runes by the hearth, Peretur sat outside on the wall bench, barefoot, enjoying the grass under her feet, eating slowly, aware of the spring breeze, and clouds scudding over-head. It would rain later. She hoped Bony and Broc were not fretting.

Nimuë came to sit by her, hip to hip. Peretur leaned her head on Nimuë's shoulder, felt her chest rise and fall: steady, determined.

"There is one more thing to try," she said.

"Then we'll try it."

"It is . . . not without risk."

Peretur laughed. Risk. Her whole life was risk. And now, today, with Nimuë at her side—and keeping food down—Peretur felt she could slay a dragon. "What must I do?"

"Sip of the lake."

She sat up. "Drink some water?"

"It's not exactly water."

"Have you drunk it?"

Nimuë nodded. "Once. To learn the secret of the steps and the chamber. It—I nearly didn't come back."

"And Myrddyn?"

She shook her head. "When he saw how it took me, he quailed. The lake sometimes has a mind of its own; there's no telling how it might treat you. I survived. But you are not wholly mortal."

"There's no other way. I'll drink."

NIMUË GAVE HER a plain wooden cup—perhaps the same cup she had used for the milk—and bade her go to the edge and dip up a cupful. "Try not to touch the water. Some people forget what they're doing or who they are for a while."

She knelt by the bank, and dipped the cup in the lake. She lifted it out, dripping. The droplets seemed long and stretched, slippery as quicksilver. When it had stopped dripping, she brought it close and looked into the water. Instead of her face, she saw her mother's. She jerked, and spilt some of the water on her foot. Immediately she heard the lake

singing to her, drawing her in, down deep, where strange, toothed eels swam, and time . . .

She felt Nimuë's hand on her shoulder, and with an effort she recalled herself.

"I'm here," Nimuë said.

Peretur took a breath, lifted the cup, and drank.

The world boiled and roiled, like a storm cloud, and a great cry rose like the cry of a gull, thin and wailing: her mother. *No, no! Go back! He will hear you. I will try hide you but he will come, oh he will come!*

The cry faded, and now Peretur found herself swooping through the air, flying, flying high over the path to the thicket, only in real life there was no path to the thicket. But here was a path, and she knew as she saw it that she had made it with her first message floated on the seeds of a dandelion.

Some way ahead of her, striding along with a spear in his hand, a man who was not a man. He was tall and broad yet moved lithe as Cath Linx. His cloak was woven of mist and song, and his hair was spun gold; he could call the wind and soothe the waves, and he drew her like honey draws a bee.

When he turned his eyes were sea green, the sea of the Overland: a wild, restless green with depths of grey. When he smiled his teeth were white and straight and strong. "A long path I've been walking to what is mine, to take and to have, a long path laid by whom I knew not."

Have. Always have, take, own.

He laughed, a great shout of a laugh. "I can't see you, path-maker, but I know you're there. Show yourself! Speak!"

She could not speak, even if she wanted.

"Ah, I forgot." He waved his hand, and her tongue was free. "So, now, speak, path-maker, and speed me on my way, for though you have made a good path, a fine path, even the son of the sea grows weary."

"Why do you follow it?" she said.

He looked about, this way and that, seeking her. "Why? So that I may reclaim what is mine. So that I may return the cup to the hall of our people, high in honour, for retrieving the greatest of the four treasures. And so that one day I may recover the other two."

Two, not three. The sword, the stone, the cup, and the spear. "Tell me of your spear."

Again, he turned this way and that, this time perhaps a little closer to where she floated. "The great spear of Lugh. The spear of light that flies true to its target."

"Then choose the cup as your target, and throw the spear."

He laughed, though his laugh seemed less pleased. "I choose not."

"Why?"

He spoke unwillingly, compelled by the geas. "The spear is not what it once was. It is . . . lessened. I was betrayed once, a long time ago, one treasure stolen from me, and much of the power of this one. But I will have it back." His voice sweetened to gold. "So show me the way, now. Show me the short path now, freely, or I will bring you down and rip out your knowledge, and I will not be gentle."

Again, the voice drew her, lower and lower. "If I—"

He hurled the spear, and she cried out as something else flew by her, and slapped her away, and she was rising, rising, faster and faster, and heard her mother's *No, you will not have it! Neither will you have the cup!* Then his cry of triumph as he dissolved to mist and flowed away, fast, faster down the path—

∽⟋⟍∽

SHE STARTED UP, wild. "My mother. He will find my mother. I must go—"

"Who?"

"Manandán, my father."

Nimuë looked drawn. "Does he know who you are?"

"I have to go!"

"Does he know?"

"He—No. He knows I made the path. He knows now that Elen lives but not that she's my mother. He knows how to find her. And it's my fault. I have to go."

"Yes," Nimuë said. "We have to go, for your mother's cry was loud enough to enter the dreams of even those with only a trace of magic. Soon the Tuath will not be the only seekers of the cup."

"Dreams?" It seemed still like early afternoon.

"You've been here two days."

∽⟋⟍∽

THOUGH PERETUR WAS on fire to leave, leave now, they took some time to plan before they set off down the lake path to Caer Leon.

The first place Peretur went was the byre. The place and the horses seethed with excitement: soon there would be adventure! She stroked Bony on the nose and patted Broc on the shoulder and told them that, yes, they were going on a journey, and to eat up, eat all they could while they could.

"Not you, too, surely!" Bedwyr, leaning against the post in a familiar pose. "Don't let Cei catch you threatening to join the quest or he'll murder you out of sheer frustration."

"Quest?"

"Where've you been? Half the fort has dreamt of the Grail—even the village healer was mumbling about it when she attended Gwenhwyfar this morning."

"The queen needed a healer?"

Bedwyr's face smoothed, as people's did when they were trying not to give themselves away. "It's nothing. Though I can't say the same for you if Cei catches you threatening to leave when you've already been the-Christ-knows-where the last two days! Where *have* you been?"

Perhaps Peretur should learn the smoothing trick, because Bedwyr saw something in her face and *tck-tck*ed in irritation.

"Another lass already? Who is it this time?"

Peretur's cheeks warmed.

"Well, whoever she is should not expect you back soon. It's bad enough that Nimuë's been gone for—"

Peretur's cheeks flamed.

Bedwyr stared. "The king's sorcerer? Saint Cadog save us! Are you quite mad? She's a heathen—not that I believe all the rantings of the priest, no; he's an ignoramus who can barely read. No, she seems a fine lady. But she'll tire of you, and when she does you'll vanish like—Well, no, perhaps not. But you'll have to leave, and this time ambushing some outlaw will not be enough to return to Caer Leon's good graces."

"I didn't ambush him."

Bedwyr sighed. "No. No, I know. It's just . . . This is a bad time to get mixed up in the uncanny. Not that there is ever a good time. And this Grail business . . . The Eingl are again bursting their bounds and on the move, and some say this time the Saessonin are with them. And if half our men are out searching for some mythical cup, we'll have a hard time of it."

"Tell me of this cup."

"Myrddyn first told the story: a great gold cup, the Holy Grail. The cup the Christ drank from at the Last Supper before he died."

"And Myrddyn wanted this cup?"

"He did. He was always filling Artos's head with nonsense. He had the bards sing of it. I'm glad he's gone, to tell the truth, though you won't catch me saying that outside these walls. A magic cup, a magic stone, a magic sword. Pah!"

"It is a fine sword."

"Caledfwylch? You have no idea. I've seen it close up, though Artos won't let any but him touch it. It shimmers like watered silk and will cut other swords as though they're cheese. Afan says he heard, once, of a sword made from a sky-stone, and perhaps that's its secret, for it never needs sharpening. Now that's my kind of magic. But a golden cup and everlasting life? Though if it truly is the cup Christ drank from . . ." He touched his cross, then sighed. "But no. It's a bard's song, no more."

"Yes," said Peretur. "Where might I find Cei?"

"I'd stay out of his way for now."

"Nonetheless."

"He's in the hall. On your own head be it!"

＊＊＊

THE HALL WAS in a ferment, crowded with what seemed like half Caer Leon and half the village—even the priest of Saint Cadog was there—all arguing.

"My queen!" the one-eyed priest shouted to where Gwenhwyfar sat on the dais with Llanza at her shoulder. "I, too, dreamt of the blessed cup!"

"Drunken fool," Cei said, not bothering to lower his voice.

"I'm not drunk," shouted the priest, his cheeks purple with burst veins.

"Not yet," Cei said. "Sit down and let your betters speak."

To Peretur's surprise the next person to speak was Modron, who stood with Angharad at her side. "People here know me." A few ayes and nods. "I serve fine ale and good food for a fair price. I am not given to fancies. But I, too, dreamt of this cup."

"The Eingl don't care how many dreams—"

"Lord Cei." Gwenhwyfar's voice sliced through the hubbub. "Let the priest and the innkeeper closer."

Cei scowled, but pointed to them and jerked his thumb in the queen's direction. Then he saw Peretur. "Oh, you're finally here? Then make yourself useful. Keep this crowd back."

She found Angharad. "Are you here making ale delivery?"

"Yes."

"Then let's set up and serve outside. Cei's paying."

WHEN PERETUR RE-ENTERED the now almost empty hall, the queen and Llanza seemed to be trying to persuade Cei of something, while the priest and Modron stood close by, waiting. Peretur beckoned a houseman—the same one who had served her and Nimuë just four days ago—and suggested he bring two jugs of ale and some cups. And with the jugs and six cups, she approached the bench.

"—me an heir, I'll take any chance," Gwenhwyfar was saying. "Any. It's the Grail. Remember what Myrddyn promised of the Grail?" She caught sight of Peretur. "And if anyone can find it, it would be Lance."

Cei swallowed his impatience as Peretur poured for the queen and Llanza. Llanza took the cups with a nod. She poured then for the priest, who clutched the cup like a lifeline, and Modron, who smiled briefly at Peretur then raised her eyebrows when she lifted her cup and smelled her own ale.

Gwenhwyfar gestured the priest and Modron closer. "I'd hear your dreams now, good people." And it was clear Peretur and Cei were not to be part of that conversation.

They moved down the bench. Cei took the cup she offered, drained it in one swallow, and held it out for a refill.

"Good idea. Get that priest drunk. Get them all drunk. The Eingl are at Deverdoeu. The sooner we can be done with this nonsense and go stop them, the better."

"Where's the king?"

"Huddled with Nimuë, who came in here not an hour since and swept him into his private chamber."

"So. You think the Grail is nonsense?"

"Of course I do, O Spear Enduring. Even Bedwyr does, too, wherever he is—talking sense into the Companions, I hope. Half of them were ready to leap on their horses and gallop off, cawing, *The Grail! The Grail!* I tell you, I don't like the way this is going." He nodded to Llanza and Gwenhwyfar, listening intently now to the priest. "Artos and Gwenhwyfar both listen to Lance. But he's hard to read. He doesn't believe Christer nonsense, but on this I don't know which way he'll jump. Artos was already under too much sway from that thrice-damned Myrddyn. And the queen is so desperate for—" He scowled into his cup. The door to the king's chamber opened. Cei straightened, put his cup down, and turned, like everyone else, towards it. The hall quieted. But it was just two housemen. Cei picked his cup up again. "I'd hoped—Oh, for all the gods' sake, what is it?"

The houseman at his elbow said, "Lord, the king requires your presence in his chamber."

Cei slammed down his cup. "About time."

The houseman coughed discreetly into his fist. "Not you, lord. Lord Peretur."

"Don't be ridiculous, man."

"My lord king was very specific, my lord."

On the dais, the other houseman was already ushering
Llanza and Gwenhwyfar towards the king's chamber.

The houseman looked attentively at Peretur. "My lord?"

"Well," Cei said. He picked up his cup, put it down again.
"Oh, go on in, pretty boy, and tell him from me that while
they blather about this thrice-damned cup, the Eingl have
taken Deverdoeu."

❧

ARTURUS SAT IN a chair with arms, knees wide and
booted feet flat on the stone floor. He did not acknowledge
Peretur when she entered; but Caledfwylch sang out to her,
and his left hand, where it rested on the hilt of the sword,
tightened. He wore mail and war boots. Nimuë stood at his
right hand, Gwenhwyfar settled to his left on a stool, and
Llanza went to stand on her left. A small brazier, recently
lit, danced with flame.

Arturus ignored Peretur and spoke directly to Gwenhwyfar and Llanza. "Nimuë knows of the Grail, and how
to get it."

Everyone looked at Nimuë. She moved forward and turned
to speak to them all. Peretur had watched her preparations—
had herself brushed that burnt-wood hair for Nimuë until
it gleamed like sable—but she was still awed. Nimuë was
a woman of no particular height, no particular grace—she
did not step like a hind, or float like a cloud; she just walked,
like any other mortal—but in her dark blue cloak, the exact
colour of her eyes, and with a thick silver band around her

forehead, she shone as if she were the queen and Arturus her attendant.

"The Grail is real and it is close. But it is well protected and the way is perilous. I will go on this quest. Those who go with me must be warded, and must not be distracted by unwarded seekers who don't understand the dangers."

Silence. Then Llanza said, "We could send the others in the wrong direction."

Arturus nodded sharply: Let it be so.

Gwenhwyfar looked at Peretur, then back to Nimuë. "Who will accompany you on your quest?"

"Peretur."

The sword sang out again, and Arturus's knuckles turned white around the hilt. "I don't trust him."

"But I do, my lord."

Unexpectedly, Gwenhwyfar said, "Any man who speaks so fondly of his mother has a good heart." She looked at Llanza.

"My lord, I have fought Peretur. I would trust his right arm."

And finally, Arturus looked at her. His eyes were tight and hard. "My heart tells me you are not who you seem. Tell me why I should send you for this most precious thing when you refuse even to tell me who you are."

Peretur set aside the call of the sword and met his gaze. "You asked me once who I was and where I was from. I never knew my father. My mother's name is Elen." She took a breath. "Elen's brother is one you know: Myrddyn."

"Myrddyn!" Gwenhwyfar said. "So that's what I saw in your face! Myrddyn's sister-son."

Arturus had not changed expression. "Why did you not say so at first?"

"I wished to be welcomed for myself, not my uncle's sake."

"A youth's pride," Nimuë said.

Arturus stared unwinking at Peretur. "Indeed, you are young. Why should I trust one so young with so great a charge?"

"Because, lord king, I am the only one who can find it."

"An untried, bare-chinned youth can do what a Companion cannot?"

Peretur said nothing.

Arturus banged his hand on his chair. "I will not trust a man who stays silent!"

The coals in the brazier shifted. "My lord," Gwenhwyfar said, "if this is the Grail, the one of which Myrddyn spoke, we need it. For the sake of the kingdom. You trusted Myrddyn, who won you one great treasure. Will you not trust his sister-son?"

Arturus stared hard at Peretur as if trying to read her heart. "Where is Myrddyn? Have you spoken to him since he left Caer Leon?"

"No, lord. I arrived not knowing he had left." Not knowing he even existed. "But I know where the cup you seek is and how it is protected, and I know even now that the one my uncle feared above all is searching for it. Unless we hurry, he will find it first."

Gwenhwyfar looked at her husband and quivered like a leashed hound with the scent.

"If you go," Arturus said slowly, "if you find this thing of power, how do I know you will not claim it for yourself? You owe no oath to me."

"I would have sworn that oath!"

Nimuë stood very still. *Calmly now, calmly.*

Peretur breathed in, and then out. "Lord king, I do not want the cup." She looked deliberately at the sword, and then at Arturus. "Nor any thing of power. All I have ever wanted is to fight for what is good and clean and bright. All I want is to know who I am and where I belong. And I belong here, lord, as a Companion."

"Do you presume to bargain with me? A cup for an oath?"

"Lord, I would bring this thing here, to Nimuë's keeping, for no reward at all."

Arturus did not seem to hear her. He caressed the pommel of his sword, head cocked, as though listening to its song. "Or is it that you don't trust a king to keep a word given in private?"

Silence.

"My lord." Gwenhwyfar's voice was gentle. "You have given no word here for any to either trust or distrust."

Arturus looked from Gwenhwyfar to Llanza to Peretur to Nimuë in despair. "How can a man know what to trust?"

It was Nimuë who said, "My lord, trust those you have always trusted."

The king looked at Llanza.

"The Eingl are on the move and the Saessonin watching and waiting. We need every strong right arm. I would trust Peretur as my brother."

He looked at Gwenhwyfar.

"It won't matter if we beat back the Eingl if we have no heir. We need the Grail."

"And only Peretur can find it," Nimuë said.

Arturus looked haggard. He said to Llanza and Peretur, "Leave us. You will have our decision."

~~~

BACK IN THE hall, people were milling about; the priest was indeed drunk; and Bedwyr was there, near the front with Cei and Geraint and Beli.

Bedwyr lifted his hand when he saw them. "I had to stop that fool Llywarch riding off, and more would have joined him if they weren't so drunk on free ale."

Cei just glared at the two of them. "Why aren't we arming? The Eingl are already at Deverdoeu! Will someone tell me what in the name of Arawn is going on?"

Llanza clapped one hand on Bedwyr's shoulder and one on Cei's. "What's going on? Our byre boy here, Peretur—he's Myrddyn's sister-son."

Cei's jaw went slack.

"Christ and all his angels!" Bedwyr looked at Peretur. "Truly?"

"Myrddyn is my mother's brother."

"So you know the truth of the Grail? It's not nonsense?"

"It's not the Christ's grail, and it's not made of gold. But it's not nonsense."

"What in all the seven hells does that mean?" Cei said.

She was saved from having to speak by Modron. "Per, all my ale's gone; Angharad says you're paying for it."

"Cei is paying for it."

Cei's face darkened to plum. "What?"

Llanza said, "Remember the Eingl. This good woman's ale stopped half your men galloping off. Cheap at any price."

"Any price? Oh no." He turned to Modron. "All gone, you say? Then we've bought in bulk, which warrants a lower price."

Modron folded her arms. "Only if agreed to beforehand. Besides, it's good ale. I could have sold it all anyway. And good ale deserves a good price."

"You'd make a pauper of your king when—"

The king's door banged open, and Nimuë came through followed by the king, then Gwenhwyfar, while an army of housemen streamed the other way into the chamber. Arturus and Gwenhwyfar sat at the high bench, with Nimuë at his right. Llanza climbed up to stand at the queen's left.

Arturus spoke in a formal voice loud enough for the battlefield. "Lady Nimuë has had a vision. Cei, you will choose and send three men to ride south and east, past Caer Gloiu, in search of the Grail."

"East?" said the priest, a bit overwhelmed by the ale and the company.

"East," said Nimuë firmly. "I have read it in the stars."

Cei sipped at his ale with some satisfaction, no doubt planning to send his three least useful men on this useless quest, and good riddance.

"The rest of us may prepare for war." Arturus stood. "Go home, good people. Counsellors, chambers."

Nimuë caught Peretur's eye: *You, too.*

Cei looked sideways at her as she walked with him and Bedwyr, but made no comment. In the chamber now were stools for all, though the king again took his chair. He surveyed his counsellors: Gwenhwyfar, Llanza, Bedwyr, Cei, Geraint, Beli . . .

"Where's my Lord Andros?"

Cei stood briefly. "About his quartermaster business, my lord. Gathering supplies for the march. For the Eingl have taken Deverdoeu, and we must march soon."

Arturus nodded. "We will." And now his voice resumed its formal tone. "Lords, ladies, the quest east is a ruse. The real quest is for three in this room; they will journey into great peril to bring the cup back to Caer Leon for safekeeping. Stand forward now, Lady Nimuë, Lord Llanza, and Lord Peretur."

Lord Peretur. She felt as though someone had pulled the bones from her legs and left her balance uncertain. She stood next to Nimuë, between her and Llanza. Llanza. Of course; sending him was one way for Arturus to be sure she brought back the cup.

The others were making approving noises: it made sense. Nimuë, a sorcerer. Llanza, the king's champion. And Peretur, sorcerer's sister-son, on horseback second only to Llanza, and, on foot, to none.

"This is a perilous journey. Those who complete it will gain high honour and full reward. Lady Nimuë's concern is not this world; her reward is not one I can bestow, though while I live she will want for nothing. Lord Llanza is my sword brother; what's mine is already his; between us there can be no reward. But for Peretur, we must offer some token. Lord Peretur, what reward would you claim?"

"None, my lord."

"Nonetheless, a king may not be seen to be ungenerous. You have long wished to be accepted as a Companion. Therefore, should you succeed and bring this most precious thing here for safekeeping, I will name you Companion to the king. What say you lords, ladies? Bear witness."

"Aye!"

PERETUR HAD NEVER travelled in company, and never with a tent and so much food. But mountain weather was chancy early in the year, and they would have no time to hunt. Nimuë rode a sturdy grey gelding, Gawr, and Llanza his black. Peretur was mounted on Broc, and led Bony as pack animal so the other mounts were not overburdened; they planned to ride hard. A great urgency was on her, and Nimuë, too, and Llanza caught it from them.

They were good travelling companions. Llanza had lived half his life in the saddle and Nimuë had journeyed far and often. Both were easy with each other, and after a while Peretur found her rhythm with them. They rode hard all afternoon—trot, canter, walk, canter, trot, walk—rarely speaking, taking hill paths Llanza and Nimuë knew but Peretur did not—for she had come to Caer Leon by a roundabout route, as much through the farming lowlands as she could. Light lingered longer in the hills so they kept going long after those in the valleys might be setting up camp. Peretur would have ridden as long as Broc was willing—*He will come, oh he will come!*—but Llanza could not see in the dark, nor their horses, and she had already sensed two wolves and one wildcat padding in the heights above them. She could persuade them away, but doing so might prove another beacon for any watching.

They made camp in a hollow against a hill that sheltered them from the wind. When Llanza would have hobbled the horses, Peretur just shook her head and spoke in Broc's ear—a quiet thing, a private thing, that would not be heard by any but the horse. "He won't let them stray out of sight," she said.

He made no comment, but she caught him looking at her now and again as Nimuë stirred the kettle and Peretur laid their bedrolls by the fire.

As the food warmed they sat quietly around the fire wrapped in their cloaks. Thick clouds covered the stars and nail-paring of a moon; the only light was the dancing red and yellow of the flame.

They talked a little of the Eingl and their habit of turning on their paymasters and taking control of kingdoms, bringing kin to settle on unused land, and gradually encroaching on others' farms. They were many now, with more coming. Arturus would find the fighting fierce, for all men fought hard for their land, and this would be the first time Arturus would face them without Llanza at his side.

"Yet you choose to be here," Nimuë said.

"He has Caledfwylch. He will prevail. And as Gwenhwyfar says, what will it matter if we turn back the Eingl but have no one to succeed Artos?"

The food was ready. They ate. And afterwards Llanza said nothing as Nimuë leaned her head on Peretur's shoulder, and Peretur put her arm around her. Peretur kissed Nimuë's hair, which smelt of the spices she ground for their milk.

"So," he said. "I will speak first of what I know. There is a cup, and you wish to find it first. Most believe it is the Grail. But it is not."

"No," Peretur said.

"But you are in a hurry to find it."

"Yes," said Nimuë.

Peretur felt the wind at her neck. *He will come, oh he will come!*

Llanza looked pleadingly at them. "If it's not the Grail, would this cup . . . Might Gwen still be made whole?"

The fire spat as a new bough caught and crackled.

"It is not a cup," Peretur said at last. "It is a bowl. It is an uncanny thing. If Gwenhwyfar drinks from it, will she get with child? Perhaps. But the getting of children depends, too, upon the father."

The sound of Nimuë's grey tearing a mouthful of grass came sudden and clear, and Peretur, between one breath and the next, was tired of deceit.

"We three around this fire have many secrets. We ride a hard road, and secrets may prove a burden. So. Llanza—Lance—my mother is indeed Myrddyn's sister, but I am not Myrddyn's sister-son."

Lance frowned. "I don't understand."

"I am not his sister-*son*."

His eyes stretched wide. He reassessed the line of her jaw, the size of her hands. She nodded.

Then he reassessed how she and Nimuë sat with each other.

This time Nimuë nodded. "So now you know something of me, too."

"Now it is your turn," Peretur said. "Tell me, why do both you and Arturus believe the trouble with an heir lies with Gwenhwyfar?"

He picked up a twig and began to strip it. "Gwenhwyfar, Gwen, has been married to Artos for some years. She has not, in all that time, conceived. She—" He threw the twig in the fire, picked up another. "For much of that time, Artos believed he had no children by other women. But I had a son not long after I left Astur and came over the sea. He is hale and being raised by the brothers at Caergybi."

"And you are Arturus's sword brother."

"And brothers share. And so."

"And so," Nimuë agreed.

He seemed relieved he would not have to spell it out. "And then we found that Artos did, indeed, have a living son. Though not one suitable for an heir. The difficulty then lies with Gwen. But we both love her." He crushed the twig in his hand. "We both love her, as we love each other. We will not set her aside."

"And then came Myrddyn."

"And then came Myrddyn with his tales of the Holy Grail, one sip from which could cure any mortal's ills. He was so persuasive that Gwen began attending the church of Saint Cadog, and praying to the Christ. And it breaks my heart to see so proud a woman on her knees begging, day after day. So I will bring this thing to her, and she will drink."

"First, we have to find it."

⸎

PERETUR WOKE BEFORE dawn, and her bones seethed with the need to hurry. She rose and cried out, "Now. We must leave now!" And such was her urgency that they saddled their horses in the dark and Lance followed them, trusting, as they rode at breakneck speed up the twisting mountain path. Broc was bigger and stronger than the other mounts, so that Peretur had to keep reining him in, and by noon when they reached the peaks and began to descend, she was twisting this way and that in a lather of impatience. She could feel Manandán's triumph as he grew closer to the cave and feel her mother's fear growing as she sensed his approach: he would take her mind, take her body and her will, take everything. The smell of burning filled Peretur's head.

They had six leagues yet to go.

"Go," said Nimuë. "We'll lighten our load and come as we can." She was already unfastening Bony's pack and letting it slide, fitting a saddle to him instead. "Ride, love."

141

With three horses between two riders, the others might catch her, or they might not. She kicked Broc, and he leapt forward.

Broc was a fine horse, the best horse, but by the time they reached the valley he was faltering, with still a league to go. She slid from his back, told him, *Rest!,* took her spear and shield, and began to run.

This was her valley. She knew every nook and cranny, every finger-width. Each time her foot hit the turf, she felt another time she had trod there, at eight, at eleven, at fourteen, and the land pushed her foot back up, and out, and on. The trees rustled for her: Elm called to the sparrowhawk, who flew the straightest path for her to follow. The blackbirds and the mistle thrush sang her on. She ran fleet as a deer. She passed the stone where she had once laid her lamb. She leapt the stream. She flew past the dog fox den and the steading where once a farmwife had blown her a kiss. She hurtled past the pond where the mallards quacked encouragement, and a bittern boomed, *On, on!* And she was drawn faster and faster by her mother's fear and Manandán's eager glee, so strong she wondered how half the world was not running like sheep before the wolf.

Then there was the thicket, seen and not seen through the blur of her mother's warding, though now overlaid with a mist. His mist: thickening, smothering, coalescing; coming.

She fought through the ward—the mindless ward saying only *No, nothing, here is nothing*—and crashed into the thicket, careless of the thorns that scored wherever her leathers did not cover. And now her mother's fear rolled and boiled,

boiled and built. *Mother, mother!* With a great cry—hers, her mother's, faraway Nimuë's—Peretur tore free of the thorns and burst bleeding into the clearing—just as the fear stilled, stopped, and began to drain away: pouring away, pouring out with her mother's life. She stumbled through the leather curtain and found her mother on the dirt floor with froth on her lips and a knife in her heart, blood still pooling about the hearth.

And, so faint it could have been the air, *Bêr-hyddur. My Bêr-hyddur. He'll not have my treasure.*

Still alive. She was still alive. The bowl. One sip, that was all it would take. Just one. But the bowl was not there. She looked about desperately.

She threw spear and shield aside and carefully, gently, slid one arm under her mother's shoulders. "Mother, the bowl. The bowl. Where is it? Quick now, oh quick."

But Elen smiled faintly. *He'll not have my treasure, no.* And the light that was her life winked out.

Her mother lay in her arms, warm and soft, and weighing nothing. So thin and worn, with fresh dirt and ash under split fingernails. And as the blood soaked through the leather at Peretur's knees, so too did the essence of Elen's life; and as mist fumed inside the cave and thickened into the shape of a man, Elen's daughter—Bêr-hyddur, spear enduring—understood everything.

She stood, heavy with grief, and met the gaze of Manandán, her father. Her own sea-grey with green to his sea-green with grey.

"You," he said. "Path-maker." He looked at the blood on

her knees, then at the pitiful small shape on the floor beside her. "Did you kill her?"

"In a way," Peretur said.

Manandán laughed. And her grief began to harden to rage. "Good," he said. "Mind, it would have saved me much grief if you had done it sooner. Though I thank you for the path that led me here. For she stole something of mine, a cup, a trifle, that I would take back." He spoke easily, as god to mortal, lord to slave: as I want a thing, so it shall be.

But they were not in the Overland now. They were in the mortal world, her world. "No."

He blinked, so like a cat sniffing cut onion that she laughed.

"Who are you to laugh at me?"

She weighed his height, his weight, his strength. "Your death." And she was reaching for her spear when he threw his.

This time there was no mother to push her aside, but this time they were not in the Overland; they were in her world. This time she could watch the spear as it came, know to a hair's width its path, see the glitter of its edge—twin to Caledfwylch's—sharp enough to part air. This time, too, she could feel its uncanny power, its craving for blood, her blood, because she was the target of the hand that threw it. But now she knew, too, what she had not known before, and she stepped to one side and called to the spear, called it to its own power: to her, where the power lived, power stolen from the spear by her mother and woven into her blood and bone. Bêr-hyddur, spear enduring.

She plucked it from the air, and smiled at her father.

But he was not there. He was Manandán, son of the sea, lord of the Tuath Dé, creature of mist and deception, and now he grew behind her, and in his hand was her own spear, Talorcan's spear of long ago, and he threw it full hard—

And she laughed, for to her the spear flowed slow as treacle, and she swayed to the side, watching the spear move past, so close she could have touched it, so slow she could have danced around it—

—just as Nimuë and Lance ran into the cave. The spear took Nimuë in the belly, and she folded down with a sigh. Lance cried out, a long, stretched sound, and reached for his sword, but even as he drew it—slowly; slow as a drawn-out note—Peretur turned and thrust the spear of Lugh through Manandán's throat. He died not believing it, trying to laugh still, for how could a mortal kill one of the Tuath?

But Nimuë was bleeding, bleeding just like Elen. Peretur fell to her knees and plunged her bare hands into the scorching ash and dirt of the hearth and started to dig.

Lance stared at the floor where a man had just fallen and was now gone, vanished as though he never was. He turned, bewildered. "What are you doing? Stop. Peretur, stop. She is dying!"

Peretur dug like a beast unhinged, and there, yes, the bowl her mother had buried in haste, so that Manandán, even if he found her before she died, could not revive her and take her mind and with it her secret, her treasure: Bêrhyddur, spear enduring.

"Water," she said harshly.

"But—"

"Water. Now." And she pushed him with her mind and showed him the spring. He ran.

"Love. Hold on for me. Hold on." She heaved the bowl free and knocked out the dirt. "Hold on. For me. Just this one thing. Hold on."

Lance ran in, his lopsided roll spilling the water from his helm, but there was enough. She poured it into the bowl. "Lift her."

So pale. Peretur dipped her hand in the bowl, cupped water, dribbled it onto Nimuë's lips. Stroked her throat. Nothing. Did it again. Saw the faintest swallow. More. A more definite swallow, and Nimuë's eyes fluttered.

Lance bent closer. "Is she . . . ? Give her more!"

Peretur shook her head. "It is enough."

❧

IT WAS THE beginning of summer, and the weather set for fair, so Peretur carried Nimuë, now in a deep healing sleep, outside and settled her comfortably in a place where the sun would remain for hours yet.

"Stay with her," she told Lance.

She unsaddled the horses—she called to Broc to come, come and eat the sweet valley grass—admonished them to not stray beyond the stream, and piled the tack in the shade.

In the cave, she knelt by her mother on the side away from the blood. The knife—Talorcan's knife—jutted out from under her ribs. It came out easily; her mother's body did not try to hold it. In the single chest her mother had brought from her other life—some kind of scented wood, beautifully painted in the old style with gods and goddesses and grapes—she found one of her old tunics, carefully folded. She shook it out—faded, worn soft with use—and tore strips from it. She wiped the blade clean with one, then set both aside. Her mother was so light that when Peretur straightened her limbs it felt like playing with a kitten. She wiped the froth from her mother's mouth and chin, then wound a strip of cloth around her eyes. She used another to bind her legs together, and tugged the dress down to cover it. After a moment she crossed her mother's arms over her chest, which hid the gaping wound. Then she smoothed Elen's hair back from her forehead.

"He did not get it," she told her mother. "He did not get your treasure. And now he is no more. He'll never hurt anyone again. And nor will your brother."

Her mother made no reply, as she would never make reply again.

The bowl seemed unchanged. Carefully, she poured away the last drops of water, then wiped it dry with the torn tunic. She sat back on her heels and contemplated it. A dangerous thing, and beautiful. Even now she longed to trace its figures with her fingertips, smooth the sharp points with her hands. It would look lovely hanging over Nimuë's hearth with stew bubbling, sending the scent stealing . . .

She wrapped it in the blanket from her mother's bed—the one they had shared when she came no higher than her mother's waist, when Elen smiled and called her Dawnged—hiding its beauty from her own longing. She carried the bundle out and tucked it under the saddles and cloths.

On the other side of the clearing, in the sun, Lance was watching over Nimuë. She was breathing slow and steady and deep, and though her cheeks were pale her lips were red, and the tips of her fingers pink.

"She's made no murmur," he said. "How long will she sleep?"

"As long as she needs."

They both watched her breathe. In and out. In and out.

"I need your help," Peretur said.

⌦⌫

ELEN SEEMED TO have shrunk even in such a short time. Or perhaps it was just the difference between watching a living woman breathe and the horrible stillness of the dead.

"Pass me the fur from the bed to wrap her in."

He looked dubiously at the bed. "It will be crawling with vermin. Such low places always are."

She stood slowly, towering over his well-fed frame wrapped in its fine leathers. "One day I shall name to you the herbs that keep vermin away. My mother used them all. And if any louse did not stay away, you would be blessed to be crawled upon by something that had touched her hem."

Lance's face turned the colour of ash. "Your mother? I— It would be an honour."

She carried her mother to the other side of the hill, and Lance followed with the sad, makeshift things they had once used as spades, and the woven willow tray her mother used to carry seedlings to the plant bed.

They took turns digging. She had chosen a spot where

the trees told her they had no thick roots, and the badgers knew to be rich with worms, and well-loosened. And her mother was a small woman. It did not take long.

Peretur climbed into the grave, laid her hands on the dirt walls, the floor—*Come. Eat, grow, let all lives be one*—then looked up to Lance. "Pass the ferns." When she was satisfied with the green carpet, she said, "Now give her to me."

She laid Elen on the ferns and covered her in fur, then laid Talorcan's knife in its sheath on her breast. Next to that went the spray of climbing rose. "This should have been your cup. I'm sorry. But we must keep it safe."

Though she did not need Lance's help to climb out, she took his offered arm. They refilled the grave together. When they were done, it was early afternoon, and Nimuë slept on. She slept still when they built a fire and Peretur broke the boar spear, red with Nimuë's blood, into three pieces. She slept as the spear burned. She slept still as the evening star slid over the rim of the hill.

They had brought no ale or wine, but the water of the stream was good with cheese and the last of the bread smeared with honey the bees had allowed Peretur to take.

"You grew up here," Lance said. "You and your mother."

"It's all I ever knew until I left for Caer Leon. She was all I knew."

"Tell me of her."

And so Peretur did. Her mother telling stories of the Tuath Dé; the good days when she was Dawnged; the bad times when she was Tâl. She spoke of the trees and the ducklings, of being blown her first kiss by that young farmwife.

It was dark by then, but she sensed Lance's smile of recognition. Then he told the tale of the young woman who had tended his wounds when he first reached these shores—lost and alone in a land where the rain seemed endless, the sun thin and pale, and the food all wrong—long before he knew Arturus; how he had left her, even though she was with child. He was ashamed but not ashamed enough to stay. He sent gifts for the boy's upkeep when he could.

"Do you see him?"

"I've met him twice, though he doesn't know I'm his father. His name is Galath, and he takes after his mother: soft skin, lighter than mine, light as toasted acorn flour, hair the colour of pine resin darkening in the sun, and eyes the red-brown of the sweet chestnuts that grow in the foothills of the mountains."

She heard the longing in his voice, even now. "I hadn't realised how much I missed this valley. And it's been only a year. How long for you?"

"A dozen years. More."

"I missed the smell of the ferns."

"What I miss most is my mother's fabada—blood sausage and beans and saffron from the south."

Peretur's mouth watered.

He nodded in the dark. "You'd like it. It's best eaten with cidra, made from sharp apples that taste of thin hill dirt and summer sun."

"Will you go back?"

"I might." But she could tell he did not believe it.

"Not with Galath?"

"The brothers of Caergybi are raising him now. I have visited the monastery twice on different pretexts. When I asked him, *Would you be happier if you had a father?* he said, *God is my father, and the monks my brothers.*" He shook his head. "They are raising him to aim for perfection."

He looked at his leg and rubbed at the knee. His own son would despise him for his imperfections. "The cup . . ."

"No," she said gently. "It is not for you."

He sighed. "It's— It would be strange after all this time to walk with no limp. And it could change how I ride."

"And when you ride you look like a centaur."

"A what?"

"A creature from my mother's scrolls." And so they passed the night telling more stories, this time none of them true.

She slept next to Nimuë and woke briefly before dawn. A summer storm grumbled and rumbled down the valley but did not reach the secret thicket. Nimuë's breathing had changed: lighter and more easy. Peretur fell asleep again, content.

After she rose, when they had added new wood to the fire and were heating water, Nimuë stirred. Peretur was there, holding her hand, when she blinked and tried to sit up.

"Easy now." She stroked Nimuë's hair, searched her face. No lines of pain. "How do you feel?"

"Famished."

"Your belly?"

"My . . . ?" Nimuë frowned. "But that was a dream." Pause. "It wasn't a dream?"

Peretur shook her head.

Nimuë looked at her belly. "Am I dying?"

"Do you feel as though you're dying?"

Nimuë, not caring about Lance, pulled aside her cloak, then the great rent in her dress. A thick white seam crossed her belly at a slant just above her navel. She touched it tentatively, then again harder. She hissed.

"Sore?"

"Not as sore as it should be."

"Would you like to sit up? I'll help."

It did seem to hurt. She panted for a moment. "What happened?"

Lance brought her a bowl of hot oatmeal. "No milk. But there's honey, or salt."

"What happened?"

"You drank of the cup."

THEY STAYED IN the clearing. Nimuë, though healed, was weak, and it would not hurt the horses to eat the good, sweet valley grass for a while. Peretur took off her mail shirt and red leathers to clean and mend and did not bother putting them back on over her undershirt and soft breeks.

Nimuë slept most of the time, and when she woke she craved food to replenish her blood, hungering for liver and sharp, fresh greens. Peretur took the spear of Lugh and went roaming. Up the hill at the farmstead, hidden from view, she watched the young farmwife with an infant at her hip, trying to cut a tree fallen across the track in the storm. But her hatchet was small, and the infant began to squall, and soon the farmwife also wept, then wiped her eyes, sat on the trunk, and opened her bodice for the infant to suckle. There was no sign of her man.

From there Peretur moved to the heights, passing the shepherd with her sheep, unnoticed by any but the shepherd's dog, who after a moment remembered her scent. As evening came she ran a while with Cath Linx and came back down the hill after dark.

The next morning, when the young farmwife took up her pitiful hatchet once more and stepped from her door, she found more wood than she could use in a year neatly stacked by her gate, along with one perfect sweet-smelling violet, and this time she wept with delight. When she had wiped her face, she went inside and brought out four barley cakes wrapped in a cloth which she put on the stump, with an exaggerated gesture that meant to anyone watching, *For you.*

The cakes were lovely with the last of their cheese.

ON THE THIRD day, Nimuë was fully alert, and it was Lance who left the thicket to hunt. Peretur told her all that had happened in the cave, exactly.

"And Lance? What does he understand?"

"Everything but that Manandán was my father. Nor does he know I ate and drank from the cup every day of my life in the cave."

"He doesn't need to know. Where is it now?"

"Hidden. And it should stay so. Like all things of the Tuath Dé, it . . . calls."

"I would see it, though," Nimuë said.

Reluctantly, Peretur brought it out and set it on the grass. Nimuë leaned forward, lips parted, then with an effort of will, sat back and linked her own hands together behind her. "Tilt it up for me." Peretur did. Nimuë started to lean forward again, then looked away. "You were right, love. It's too beautiful. Take it away. Hide it."

She did.

When she got back, she sat behind Nimuë and wrapped her arms around her.

"The bowl's iron has the same shine as Artos's sword," Nimuë said.

Peretur nodded against her head. "The same as the blade on the spear of Lugh. My spear now."

Nimuë turned in her arms. "Is that wise?"

"Its power is now wholly in me. But the blade is very sharp, and it flies true."

"The power is in you?" Nimuë's red lips curved. "Is that why you are so burnished and beautiful? Why you call so to me . . ."

Peretur kissed her.

Some time later, Nimuë said drowsily, "I hope Lance brings something bigger than a bird, I'm famished. And I hope it's soon."

The sun was slanting. Peretur sat up. "He's been gone a long time." She pulled on her undershirt, thinking of Talorcan's bones on the lonely fell. But, no, Lance was on foot. He was lithe, well-knit, and well-armed. Nimuë handed Peretur her breeks, and shook out her own dress with its rough repair down the front.

"I don't want to leave you unguarded."

"I have my own protections," Nimuë said. "They would not see me."

Peretur stared, then laughed, and kissed her. "This won't take long. Stay right there."

She loped away, and there, fifty paces beyond the thicket, sitting with his back towards the thorns, sat Lance with a brace of hares.

"Lost?"

He whipped around and scowled. "Where did you come from?"

She pointed to the thorns.

He peered, said crossly, "What are you pointing at?"

She grinned. "Here. Put your hand on my shoulder and I'll show you."

∾⊷⊷

OVER A STEW of hare and onions and carrots, scented with thyme and rosemary, Lance told them of going round and round in circles.

"Did you call out?" Peretur asked. She had never thought to wonder if her mother's ward also shut out sound.

"I did. And trust me when I say you should be glad you couldn't hear some of the things I shouted."

"How long will Elen's ward last?" Nimuë asked.

"I don't know. Many years, perhaps. It was bound with more than ordinary mortal strength, and has been renewed over and over until it's woven into the very fabric of the hill." Then she saw what Nimuë was thinking. "No, love. We can't leave the cup here. Manandán found his way even when she was alive and strong. It is too dangerous."

"It will be safe at Caer Leon," Lance said.

"No," said Peretur.

"But—"

"No," Nimuë said. "You saw what happened."

Lance looked stubborn.

Nimuë set aside her bowl, unpicked the stitches in her dress, and pulled it aside. "Look, Lance. You've seen spear wounds. Now look at it."

Unwillingly, he looked.

"How could any king resist drinking of the cup to cure himself of such a wound?"

"Why should he resist? Artos is a good king," he said.

"I would have died. And now three days later I am healed."

"Artos is a good king," Lance said again.

"Yes," Nimuë said. "A good king because he has a strong vision. A vision he believes will make the world a better place—as do we all, which is why we serve him. A good king, with a good vision. But if he believed himself invulnerable, what risks would he take in service of that vision? And how long after that before he stopped listening to the counsel of others? Mortals should be mortal."

"A man's immortality should be through his children," Peretur said. "With a single, small sip, Gwenhwyfar's difficulties can be healed. This is why we came for the cup." Or at least why Arturus sent them.

"But the cup doesn't have to be in Caer Leon for that,"

Nimuë said. "And you will help us persuade Artos and Gwenhwyfar of this."

"He is not an easy man to persuade."

. "No, which is why we will take it directly to the lake. You will go into Caer Leon itself and explain to Artos and Gwenhwyfar how it must be. And if they do not agree I will know it, and my gate will never open for them again. They will never again come to the lake, Gwenhwyfar will never get to drink, and there will be no heir."

THEY PLANTED FORGET-ME-NOT seeds over Elen's grave where birds would sing, and left the cave tidy and supplied with firewood, scrolls neatly laid in the fine chest, just in case some traveller, someday, found her way through the ward and needed a refuge for a while. Then with the dew still heavy on the grass, they rode out, their horses' hooves leaving a dark trail through the silver.

This time they travelled the easier, longer lowland road. Peretur and Lance both wore their mail shirts over their leathers. For the first two days, they rode in high spirits: the weather was fine, the hunting was good, and they and their horses were in fine fettle. Every now and again Peretur would point out a track leading to an isolated farmstead where she had worked for a day or a week, and once the mean and ramshackle dwelling where she had found Bony. But they were content to sleep under the stars and keep their own company.

The third day dawned grey and uncertain; sound carried strangely. They stopped at midday, turned the horses loose to graze, and divided the meat they had caught and cooked the night before.

"The horses are restless," Lance said.

"Weather's changing," Peretur said. "It'll rain later. We should hunt before then."

Lance sighed, then sighed again at the half-raw, half-scorched meat in his hand. "I would hunt a herd of wild loaves."

Nimuë nodded. "And egg-laying chickens."

"And a milk cow."

"Milk," Nimuë and Lance both said with the same longing.

Peretur leaned back on her hands, surveying the slope of the land. "The horses could do with something more than grass." She looked this way and that. Yes. "There's a steading four leagues from here. Well run. Bigger than others we've passed. They may have eggs and bread to trade. We might have to sleep in the byre, but it's a good byre. And the farmwife is friendly." She smiled, remembering sneaking away in the dead of night with Bony when that same wife, *Call me Blodwen,* had made hot eyes at her, and the weeks of dreams after.

"Anything to avoid sleeping in the rain. And to breakfast on bread and milk and eggs!"

The rain began just as they climbed back in the saddle. At first it was light, but then it came down in earnest and they had to slow to a walk because they could not see more than two yards ahead; the track became a sea of mud. They had cloaks, and Nimuë's hood kept off the worst, but both

Peretur and Lance rode without hoods in order to keep their side vision. They plodded on grimly, hair plastered to their heads and rain trickling down the backs of their necks. It grew darker as the clouds thickened. Twice, they had to take shelter when the sky loosed a torrent. Each time they set out again, they moved more slowly than before.

It was growing dark when they rode into the farmyard, and still the rain sheeted down. A dog barked. Peretur sent a greeting, and it quieted.

They reined in. "Stay there. I'll go find the farmer and ask where we can bed down."

She led Broc around to the back door and thumped with her mailed fist. No reply. She thumped again, a little harder.

The door opened. The farmer brandished a great stick in one hand and a burning brand with the other. "Be off with—" Then the torchlight hit Peretur's armour, glinted from her sword hilt, glowed on the red of her leather, and the man dropped his shoulders, lowered his gaze, and spoke to the floor. "Lord, oh beg pardon, lord."

Peretur blinked. "It's fine," she said. "We're just three travellers hoping to sleep in your byre out of the rain."

"Rhys?" A woman's voice. "Close that thrice-cursed door."

But the farmer seemed frozen.

"Rhys! We've wind blowing in like the breath of Annwn itself. Oh, for—"

And there she was, Blodwen of her dreams, Blodwen of the curved red mouth and bright brown eyes, and inside her mailed gauntlet Peretur remembered the feel of her breast under her palm. She smiled and stepped forward. "Blodwen."

But Blodwen, like her husband, seemed to deflate like a pricked bladder; her eyes dulled and she too looked down. "Lord."

"Don't you remember me, Blodwen?"

"If you say so, lord."

"I worked here. Helped in the field."

"Yes, lord," she said woodenly, and Peretur realised she could say, *I'm the one who turned into a dragon* or *I ate your horse,* and both she and her husband would agree, because it never paid to disagree with a rich and well-armed lord. It was safest to just give them whatever they wanted and hope they would go away soon and never come back.

"Peretur?" Nimuë with Lance behind leading the horses.

Blodwen curtseyed to the floor and Rhys went down on one knee, but not before Peretur saw a flash of panic in his eyes. Peretur looked at the farmwife with her wind-roughened cheeks and plain tabby-weave dress, patched and stained, then at Nimuë's thick cloak, sleek hair, and glint of gold at wrist and cheek. If a lord was frightening, a noble lady was terrifying.

"Is there a problem, love? Can we sleep in the byre or not?"

"Byre?" Rhys said, horrified, at the same time that Blodwen stood aside and said, "Our poor house is yours, lady. Rhys, see to their honours' horses."

Rhys looked as though he was terrified of touching such valuable beasts, and Peretur was unwilling to let the bowl away from her hand until it was safe at the lake. Yet they thought her a lord; only peasants tended horses in the byre.

She felt as though she stood with one foot on the riverbank, the other on a boat, and they were moving apart.

"Come, man," she said finally. "We will do it together."

In the byre, which was much smaller than she remembered, Rhys stayed terrified, uncertain what to do, and the horses began to roll their eyes and shy, so in the end, for the horses' sake, and Rhys's, she behaved as expected, the way that made him comfortable: she ignored him except to give orders.

When they mounted up the next morning she sat high on Broc, and pretended not to see the swiftly hidden resentment on Blodwen's face when she exchanged a soft leather sack of silver coin for a basket of bread and cheese she knew was worth no more than ten coppers. And when they rode away she knew she was leaving part of her life forever, riding from Per, from Tâl and Dawnged, riding to Peretur Paladr Hir, Spear Enduring; Lord Companion, and Beloved of the king's sorcerer.

THE LATE AFTERNOON sky over the lake this time was grey, but the water laughed and sparkled, reflecting the blue sky and summer sunshine of some other time and place. Peretur watched the flickers of light and thought perhaps her mother looked down from that place, giving her blessing. She lifted her hand and waved a last farewell. Then she went in and closed the door.

Arturus, Gwenhwyfar, Llanza, and Nimuë were already gathered before the black iron bowl upon the elm table. She joined them.

"My lords," Nimuë said formally. "Lady. One small sip, no more. And only for the queen. Then the bowl will be given to the lake and hidden forever from mortal sight." She picked up a small silver cup. "Do you agree?"

Gwenhwyfar took Arturus's hand in her right and Llanza's hand in her left. "I agree."

Nimuë looked at Arturus, then Llanza, who both nodded.

"Very well. Peretur?"

Peretur stood before them, touched each on the forehead and murmured as she would to a horse, as Nimuë turned to the bowl. Then Peretur stepped away, and Nimuë held the dripping cup to Gwenhwyfar.

She took it solemnly in both hands, and sipped, once, then gave the cup back to Nimuë and closed her eyes. "It is so cold," she said, and paled a little.

Both men put a protective arm around her. "Take her to the hearth," Nimuë said. "Keep her warm. I'll bring something."

Peretur occupied them all by fussing with a thick blanket, and reminding them again of the need for their silence, laying an earnest hand on each shoulder as she spoke. Then they were sipping spiced ale, while Nimuë wiped the bowl dry as a bone and laid the damp cloth ceremonially on the fire to burn.

By the time the three had reached the end of their cups, they were gazing moon-eyed at one another, and it was clear to Peretur that they might not be able to wait to start trying to make an heir.

"The queen may be very tired," Nimuë said. "She may need bed very soon, and her own bed would be best."

Yes, they all agreed. Very soon. The sooner the better.

"I will see you safely down the path," Peretur said, and took up her spear, which went with her now everywhere.

෨෮෨

THEY SET THE bowl on the slab of liver-coloured stone at Myrddyn's feet. Myrddyn no longer looked young but old and thin, dry as a stick. As they watched, a hank of his shining bronze hair fell out.

With the death of his sister, the source of his power had died, and even the stone could not bind him to life. Soon he would be nothing but bones, then dust. And in time the sword would take his place.

෨෮෨

IT WAS DARK when they closed the door to the rock chamber. Peretur propped the great spear of Lugh against the doorjamb like a broom, next to her shield, painted now with a Companion's sigil—for her, a spear—and they settled themselves by the fire with a jug and two cups.

"Did we do right?"

"We did," Peretur said. "Though it would have been a beautiful baby."

They both sighed. But it had to be: any man or woman with a child yearns to give that child every advantage. If Artos had a son or daughter to pass the sword to, all the vows in the world would not persuade him to give it up when it was his time.

"What did you put in that cup? I thought she would faint."

Nimuë got up, reached under the table, and brought out the other, hidden bowl and the silver cup. She peered into it. "There's not much left. She took a much bigger sip than she should have." She handed it to Peretur. "See for yourself."

Peretur sipped, rolled the water round in her mouth. "Spearmint?"

"Mint will make water feel cold. The rest was in her mind."

Nimuë poured them cups of the spiced ale, handed one to Peretur. They sipped. "And what's in this? Whatever it is, I just hope they haven't already rutted themselves to death. Or is that all in their heads, too?"

"Oh, no. No, these spices are quite real. Quite effective."

They both sipped, feeling the warmth coursing through their veins and pooling in their bellies. Nimuë stroked her hair. "I wish I could have met your mother."

They sipped and talked. The quest for the Grail would go on, of course. Gradually Lance and Gwen and Artos would forget they had found it, forget they had supposedly drunk from it. In a few years the memory of the Eingl's defeat at Deverdoeu would fade, and they would come again. And again. And one day Artos would not be able to turn them back.

"Why does he hate them so?"

"He doesn't hate them. He hates that there are so many

of them. And he hates what they stand for: the rule of might and not the rule of law. At least not the law as he understands it. And they do not read, or write, or build with stone." She took another sip. "I have met some of them."

"What are they like?"

"Like us—they *are* us. Or their forebears were, though now they follow the dress and customs of those who first came over the sea to fight for the Redcrests against the Picts and Scots. And now what was the common trade tongue is their only tongue; they have forgotten all others. So while their clothes are different from ours, and their weapons and food, their hearts are the same. They fall in love. They worry about the weather and their crops. They try to make their homes beautiful. And some of them are, though it's a beauty of living things: wood and wool. Their weaving is very fine—they make a red you would love. But Artos doesn't care for their carvings or their hangings; he cares only that they don't speak his tongue, in word or belief. And he believes so strongly in his rule of law that he will do almost anything to make it happen. He will fight endlessly—but in the end he is only mortal. And there will be no heir."

"He won't change his mind about the son he has?"

"Medrawd? No. Artos will not see him, nor permit others to. For him, Medrawd represents some secret shame. It is the only thing we may not talk about."

Arturus king would die, and with no heir his legacy would fade and become nothing but a story, like the Grail, like the stone and the sword and the Tuath Dé.

"And us?" Nimuë said. "Will we fade? You are not wholly mortal, and I have drunk from the cup."

"I don't know," said Peretur. And for now, she did not care. She cared only for the fact that she was young and strong, her love was in her arms, the fire was warm, and the tide of life was rising, rising within her.

AUTHOR'S NOTE

ORIGINS

Peretur, Peredur, Peredurus, Perceval, Parzival, Percival, Parsifal—there are tales of the hero I call Peretur written in Old Welsh, Middle Welsh, Latin, Old French, Middle High German, Middle English, and a dizzying number of modern languages. And before anyone wrote such things down there were no doubt tales told in Brythonic—the P-Celtic language spoken on the British mainland before Rome invaded—and then in one of its successors, Primitive Welsh.

The first written mention is from the sixth century, in Old Welsh, with Peretur, one of the sons of Eliffer, a hero of Yr Hen Ogledd (the Old North)—so most likely a northern princeling up around Hadrian's Wall. In one genealogy, *Historia Peredur,* the name Arthur is also mentioned (Arthur as a name crops up a few times among northern British aristocracy during the Early Middle Ages[1]). Peredur appears in many poems of the period, including *Ymddiddan Myrddin a Thaliesin,* an imaginary conversation between the poet Taliesin and an early iteration of Merlin in which Peredur is praised by implication as one of the "brave sons of Eliffer" who died in a battle: so, again, a northerner. In a later (that is, more recent) recension of *Y Gododdin,* the tale of the tragic slaughter of British warriors that brings about the death of the Old North, possibly originally composed in the sixth century, Peredur is listed as one of the dead warriors.

In these early texts, then, Peretur seems to be a northern noble—but things are rarely as they seem. Not one of those works I've mentioned exists in its original form; all have been written, rewritten, translated, added to, and altered over the centuries. They also borrow from each other. So, for example, some scribe writing down the umpteenth version of Y *Gododdin* remembers having seen the name Peredur in *Annales Cambriae* (*AC*) and, for added verisimilitude, sticks the name into a list of those who died in the sixth-century battle. Yet that version of the *AC* they cribbed from was itself perhaps similarly embellished in previous eras. None of these early poems, genealogies, and annals are reliable—but all are fantastic fuel for the imagination and served as source material for later writers.

In the early twelfth century, writing in Latin, Geoffrey of Monmouth composes three works of interest: *Prophetiae Merlini* (*Prophecies of Merlin*)[2]; *Historia Regum Britanniae* (*HRB*, the *History of the Kings of Britain*); and *Vita Merlini* (*Life of Merlin*), a poem. *HRB* is a stirring pseudo-history covering about two thousand years from the founding of Britain by Brutus of Troy through to the seventh century, with some lovely just-so stories along the way about how London got its name, and so on. It's a wildly improbable hotchpotch of names and events drawn from a variety of earlier sources including Gildas, Bede, and "Nennius"[3], and decorated with generous dollops of imagination and myth. It is in *HRB* that we encounter Peredurus, a British king ruling somewhere north of the Humber and one of the powerful men who is present at a court Arthur convenes in the "City of Legions." And in *Life of Merlin,* we meet Peredur, a Northern Welsh prince.

A Norman poet, Robert Wace, translates[4]—or perhaps "loosely interprets" might be more accurate—*HRB* into a dialect of Old French, along the way inventing the famous Round Table and changing the name of Arthur's sword Caliburnus to Excalibur.

A few decades later, in five major works written in Old French, Chrétien de Troyes introduces a whole raft of characters and events that have since become pillars of Arthurian legend, for example Lancelot[5], and Perceval's search for the Grail[6]. Chrétien's Perceval is raised in the wilds of Wales by his mother; he encounters a group of knights and yearns to be one; he sets off for Arthur's court, where a girl predicts greatness for him; Sir Kay laughs at that and slaps the girl; Perceval stonks off swearing revenge; he kills a knight in red armour; decides to go see his mother and along the way encounters the Grail but does nothing about it; finds out his mother is dead; fights Sir Kay and breaks his arm; and becomes a Knight of the Round Table.

Then, in the thirteenth century Wolfram von Eschenbach pens *Parzival* in Middle High German, borrowing heavily from Chrétien, in which Parzival actually wins the Grail, becoming the new Grail king.

At this point our trail moves back to Wales, where *Peredur Son of Efrawg,* one of the Three Welsh Romances, is written in Middle Welsh.[7] There are all kinds of arguments about the story's original composition—ranging from the twelfth to the fourteenth century—and whether the author(s) cribbed from Chrétien or perhaps drew from a shared source. But once again Peretur is associated with the Old North (the name of his father, Efrawg, is a Brythonic name for York). But his father isn't important because, again, Peretur is raised in the wilds by his mother. Again he encounters knights of Camelot; again he sets off on adventures, though this time he encounters not the Grail but a severed head on a plate; the knight who makes fun of him is Cei, and we get a name for the woman Peretur loves: Angharad Golden-Hand.[8]

And finally (for my purposes) we have Thomas Malory, whose fifteenth-century Middle English epic, published in 1485 by William Caxton as *Le Morte d'Arthur*,[9] brilliantly synthesises previous sources in Britain and Europe—and is basically responsible for the legend we know today. His work overtook all others in popularity for the simple reason that it was one of the first books printed. This is how I encountered King Arthur and Camelot.

CHOICES

I first read *Le Morte d'Arthur* as a nine-year-old and fell headlong into the legend. Beneath its visible High Medieval trappings I could smell the hidden iceberg of ancientness; practically taste the moors with menhirs looming from the mist; feel the dark forests tangled and forbidding at the side of the road; and hear the forlorn cries of the lost, lonely, and mad. Even then I think I sensed that there was no single true tale of Arthur and Camelot: the legend is and always has been mythic fanfic, endless mash-ups of what has gone before, woven together and cut and draped by each writer to suit the current fashion.

Scenting a trail, I read every version I could find—I still do—but I never considered making my own contribution. As a result, I had no dog in the origin fight: all story lines, characters, and eras seemed to me equally valid, as did academic arguments regarding the legend's beginnings (though I admit to a leaning towards Arthur-as-deity). But then Swapna Krishna and Jenn Northington invited me to contribute to an anthology of "gender-bent, race-bent, LGBTQIA+ inclusive short-fiction retellings" they were putting together for Vintage. I had planned to say no—I was in the middle of writing my novel *Menewood* and didn't want to set it aside for a short story—but with my fingers poised over the keyboard to send my regrets, an image of a figure in red on a bony gelding in the woods dropped into my head and, *Oh,* I thought. *I can do something with that. . . .*

The clues were all in the initial image. The bony gelding spelled poverty, or at least a sense of mix-and-make-do: this was not a person of privilege. Then there were those woods, and wearing red—like the Red Knight of Chrétien's *Perceval,* though this figure was not exactly a knight.[10] Yes, it had to be Peretur/Peredur/Perceval/Percival! But that red . . . It wasn't plate armour, so we weren't talking a Knightly Romance; it gradually came into focus as red leathers, sewn with a mix of rings and small plates. And, oh look, there were no stirrups. So it had to be an earlier era—Peretur or Peredur—because although stirrups were used on and off in Britain from about the third century, by the end of the eleventh they were uniformly used by mounted fighters.[11] And given that the real Arthur (if there ever had been a real Arthur—which for my fictional purposes clearly there must have been) had to have been lost from history for a reason, it made sense for it to be during a time when history went largely unrecorded, that is, my favourite period: the Early Medieval.

As for the Welsh setting, that was never even a question. Although the very earliest mentions of Peretur seem equally divided between northern British or Welsh ancestry, later tales all weigh in on the Welsh side of the balance—and if even French writers like Chrétien call Peretur Welsh, why not go with the flow? Second, I wanted Wales—Dyfed, specifically—for its connection to the Irish legend of the Tuath Dé.[12]

Arthur and the Tuath Dé seem to have a lot in common; to my mind, they belong together. I suspect that both began as deities who gradually acquired human characteristics such as lust, cunning, bravery, greed, and jealousy. Certainly the Tuath Dé are a quarrelsome lot, forever stealing from one another—particularly their Four Treasures: the cauldron, the sword, the stone, and the spear. The first three treasures, in the guise of the Grail, Excalibur, and the stone Excalibur is pulled from, fit very nicely into Arthurian legend. The spear, though, on first glance? Not so much. However, once I really started paying attention to Peretur I realised that, etymologically, in Old Welsh, Peretur could be

Bêr-hyddur, "spear enduring." In other words, Peretur could *be* the spear.[13]

Given the Welsh setting, Camelot became Caer Leon. In *HRB,* Peredurus meets Arthur in the "City of Legions," and Roman Britain had three permanent legionary fortresses— Eboracum, Deva Victrix, and Isca Augusta—settlements now known as York, Chester, and Caerleon. After that it was easy: the place where Peretur grew up had to be Ystrad Tywi, the eastern border of old Dyfed that in the sixth century became a liminal space between kingdoms, particularly the less accessible northern valley.

So now I was set: Peretur, the spear, the Tuath Dé, Ystrad Tywi in the early sixth century, and travel to Arthur at Caer Leon. The rest fell into place in a feverish three-week writing sprint during which I took enormous delight in following that most honourable of Arthurian traditions: stealing blithely from all and sundry—Merlin, the Lady of the Lake, the Red Knight, the search for the Grail—and making it my own.

Even though a book stuffed with magic, gods, monsters, and legendary heroes is not by any stretch of the imagination a historical novel, I wanted the details—including the material culture for which we have archaeological evidence—to be historically grounded.[14] All the names are rendered as closely to sixth-century versions as I could manage—the ogham and Latin inscriptions on the commemorative stones, for example, are real, and found in Dyfed. The Cup, too is based on the Iron Age hanging bowls I've always admired. Given the lavish decoration of some found as grave goods, I suspect they may have acquired ritual overtones in various times and places. So the hanging bowl Peretur knows became a combination of the Gundestrup Cauldron and bowls from Sutton Hoo, York, Lullingstone, and Wilton.[15]

The fortifications—bank and ditch and palisade with some stone courses—are how I imagined Isca, the fortress and vicus, might have looked three hundred years after II Augusta withdrew. The arms and armour were a little trickier: in a world with many cultures, levels of technology, and access to same, the accoutrements of war would have varied considerably. How they were used, too, would differ from place to place. Blades, for example, were expensive in terms of time and resources, and few would have the expertise to create them new. Each blade would be valued by the owner; each would be repurposed, rehilted, and redecorated to suit changing requirements. At any one time, a body of fighting men and women might be armed with long swords, curved swords, short swords, and knives ranging from six to twenty inches. Armour, well, it would depend, again, on resources and cultural allegiance and method of fighting. Warriors could have worn anything from quilted warrior jackets, to leather sewn with panels of horn or metal, to coats of ring mail, to iron plates on legs or backs—or any combination thereof. Shields and spears—again, an enormous variety. But there have always been slim javelins (with or without soft iron points designed to bend) and big-game spears with broad thrusting blades and crosspieces designed to stop a charging boar. I had fun coming up with ways an ignorant self-taught user with superstrength might "misuse" found tools, and grinned as I imagined the beefy, arrogant Cei trying to re-create some Roman tactics only to have his nifty methods absolutely destroyed by the self-taught spear-wielder.[16]

Most importantly for me, historical accuracy also meant this could not be a story of only straight, white, nondisabled men. Crips, queers, women and other genders, and people of colour are an integral part of the history of Britain—we are embedded at every level of society, present during every change, and part of every problem and its solution. We are here now; we were there then. So we are in this story. In addition, as I don't much care for stories that are only concerned with those at the pinnacle of power, privilege, and prestige, that's not who I wrote about.[17] *Spear* became not a traditional Hero's Journey—the story of a Supremely Selfish Superhero with no mother who does everything for and by himself, and who, in relentless pursuit of his goal, which is to win, strews his path with wreckage and weeping, then returns home unchanged—but something between an ur-Bildungsroman and a truer Hero's Journey.[18] As in the early folktales in which an orphan or otherwise unwanted son (it's always a son) sets out to seek his fortune, Peretur does set out to find her place in the world, but she does it unprovoked by loss. Her mother is still very much alive; her mother and her past are not something she wants to forget—just as she is not unloved, unwanted, or unadmired at home. And though, like all heroes, Peretur does set out to win, winning for her is not a binary, a zero-sum game in which winners win and losers lose: she can win without someone else losing.

Winning for Peretur is not just about triumphing over enemies and slaying monsters—which of course she does—but
about learning, changing, and growing. Her journey is not
linear but circular: she revisits her past and the people in it.[19]
The main difference between Peretur's Journey and a traditional Hero's Journey is that her real goal is connection: finding her people and a place to belong; finding happiness—for
herself and others—at least for now.

NOTES

1. What used to be called the Dark Ages—the fifth, sixth, and
   early seventh centuries, during which in England no annals,
   no chronicles, no histories were kept because the populace was
   functionally illiterate—is now variously termed the sub-Roman
   or Late Antique or Early Middle Ages period, depending on
   one's perspective. My affinity has always been with the sixth
   and seventh centuries and I tend to prefer Early Medieval.

2. Apparently Geoffrey's Merlin prophesies launched the Gal-
   fridian tradition of political prophecy.

3. All, like Geoffrey himself, monks, and all writing with very
   particular agendas—and, in turn, pulling their information
   from dubious sources and/or one anothers' work:

   - *De Excidio et Conquestu Britanniae*: Gildas, a monk born in
     Scotland and educated in Wales, writing in—probably—the
     early sixth century, creates not a history but a sermon and
     polemic. While he discusses battles between Britons and
     "Saxons," including one at Badon, and the triumphs of one
     Ambrosius Aurelianus (repurposed by Mary Stewart—in

The Crystal Cave—as the father of Merlin), he makes no mention of Arthur or any other familiar Arthurian characters.

- *Historia Ecclesiastica Gentis Anglorum*: Bede, born in Old English–speaking Northumbria in the late seventh century and writing in the Latin of early eighth century, creates what some consider the foundation of English history. The contemporary accounts are probably quite accurate (though he left out many things that might have proved awkward for his agenda). The early history, though, is only as accurate as his sources—such as *De Excidio*. Bede, too, mentions the Battle of Badon; he also makes no mention of Arthur.

- *Historia Brittonum*: "Nennius," another monk writing in—perhaps—the early ninth century (though this is widely believed to be a misattribution; no one knows his, or her, real name), compiles a sort-of history from sources such as Gildas and Bede. Here is where we encounter Arthur and his famous twelve battles (including Mount Badon) against the Anglo-Saxons. Though I don't believe he talks about Peretur.

4. Most probably around the middle of the twelfth century.

5. *Lancelot, le Chevalier de la Charrette* (*Lancelot, the Knight of the Cart*)

6. *Perceval ou le Conte du Graal* (*Percival, or the Story of the Grail*), in which Percival, described as "the Welshman," finds the Grail—though he does nothing about it, merely observing mutely.

7. The Three Welsh Romances are part of the Mabinogion (a collection of eleven of the earliest stories of Britain, divided into Four Branches, written down in Middle Welsh but most probably composed and endlessly reinterpreted for a long time before that)—as is the tale of *Culhwch ac Olwen*, another text

that mentions Arthur but whose origins many believe predate Geoffrey of Monmouth. And of course one of the branches of the Mabinogion, *Manawydan fab Llŷr,* concerns the person Peretur knows as Manandán—an import from Irish myth.

8. Angharad Golden-Hand: I changed it to Angharad Ton Felen, "most beloved golden-waved" (that is, golden-haired), which was the name of the daughter of Rhydderch Hael, a king of Alt Clut—bringing in that northern connection yet again.

9. Clearly Caxton either couldn't spell or didn't understand French grammar.

10. Writing ideas, and the images that accompany them, are, for me, rather like dream images: I know things about what they mean without being able to say why.

11. Roman alae, or some of them, used stirrups. So the use of stirrups and different types of saddle in Britain would have depended on geography, cultural spread, and access to the necessary resources.

12. The Irish raided and settled West Wales during the fourth and fifth centuries. By the end of the fifth century, they ruled Dyfed.

13. Primitive Welsh grew from Brythonic by perhaps the mid-sixth century. By the begining of the ninth it had become Old Welsh, which sometime in the early twelfth century evolved into Middle Welsh.

14. The more a reader is able to verify details in some places, the more likely they are to willingly suspend their disbelief in others.

15. I forwarded pictures for Rovina Cai, the illustrator, and she did a wonderful job; the cauldron is just right—ditto with the armour.

16. I imagined Cei as the kind of English rugby player I used to know: mostly kind—if he thinks you're like him; not stupid

but lazy and willing to learn only when prodded; and (mostly) just this side of being an asshole but (almost) always very close to the line. Basically, a jerk but with some good points, and useful in a fight. I've spent a lot of time in a lot of pubs with men like Cei.

17. The west and southwest of Britain maintained a thriving trade with the Mediterranean, and then Constantinople and the Byzantine Empire, long after the "fall" of the Western Roman Empire, as evidenced by surviving material culture—amphorae, coinage, jewellery, etc.—and also in the fact that parts of the country suffered terribly during the earliest waves of Justinianic Plague. Before that, of course, Britain was an integral part of the Roman Empire, with merchants, civilian citizens, government officials, and military personnel from Africa, Europe, and Asia. In the book, I imagined Bedwyr as coming to Caer Leon from near Hadrian's Wall where many numeri and foederati from all over the Empire were stationed during the fourth century when Irish Pictish and Saxon raids were particularly severe. These soldiers would have intermarried with the local populace. When the Roman tax structure began to wither, those groups would have become, gradually, more like local lords, extracting payment in kind. Bedwyr's forebears were from Africa originally, but he would have grown up speaking Brythonic and Latin, perhaps with the accent of a northerner: in this sense he's as British or "Welsh" as Cei. (Though "Welsh" comes from *wealh*, an Old English word for foreigner, or slave—and that's a whole other story.) Llanza, on the other hand, is an Astur. The Astures were a Celtic tribe from Northern Spain; Llanza would have spoken a dialect of P-Celtic similar to Brythonic, but with an accent.

Andros, though, would be a native Greek speaker: his accent would definitely be marked.

18. And absolutely not a "Heroine's" Journey. I hate that word, hate it with the heat of a thousand fiery suns—it's as bad as Authoress, or Actress, or Poetess. Just . . . no. That's the problem with binaries: like old-school heroes, one is always Good and the other Bad.

19. But as Tolkien understood, Heroes can rarely go home again.

ACKNOWLEDGEMENTS

All Arthurian tales owe their existence to previous iterations. This is my first try at reworking the material and as such is heavily informed by the work of other novelists—Geoffrey of Monmouth, Thomas Malory, Bryher, Henry Treece, J. R. R. Tolkien, Rosemary Sutcliff, T. H. White, Mary Stewart, Susan Cooper, Gillian Bradshaw, Jack Whyte, and many others whose impact is probably unconscious. Then there are academics too numerous to mention but most definitely including Alex Woolf, Guy Halsall, Andrew Breeze, and Caitlin Green.

If I continue this story, the new fiction will no doubt be influenced by those whose work I encountered after finishing *Spear,* such as Tracy Deon, Bernard Cornwell, and every single contributor to Jenn Northington and Swapna Krishna's wonderful anthology, *Sword, Stone, Table.*

In fact, this book pretty much owes its existence to Jenn and Swapna. I've always loved the Matter of Britain but had never considered working with it—I thought it had all been done before—until they invited me to contribute to an anthology they were putting together for Vintage. There was just one problem: after three weeks' work, instead of the requested 8,000–10,000 words, I had the first draft of what you're reading now. Obviously, given the length, it wouldn't

ACKNOWLEDGEMENTS

work in an anthology, so I apologised and gave the money back. Jenn and Swapna were very kind about it and generous, too, in their encouragement of my own project.

But a book is more than an idea; it is also a physical object that exists in commercial space. In order to turn this idea into something you can hold in your hands, I relied upon a team.

It began, as always, with Stephanie Cabot, my agent at Susanna Lea Associates. (Thanks also to Noa and Susanna and everyone else at SLA for getting behind my work and pushing.) She took it to Sean MacDonald at FSG, who read it, liked it, but knew himself and his house well enough to acknowledge it might be a better fit elsewhere under the Macmillan roof. So he roped in his right hand, Daphne Durham, who talked to Irene Gallo, publisher of Tordotcom. Eventually everyone agreed that *Spear* would fit nicely there but that it should have an FSG editor. Enter Lydia Zoells.

This is the first time I've worked with Lydia, who is sharp, organised, helpful, energetic, thoughtful, and knowledgeable, a history geek and Arthur fan—practically perfect for this project. She and the team at Tordotcom made what could have been a bumpy collaboration supremely smooth; they are amazingly transparent, organised, and efficient, and they know their audience to a T. Every single person I've encountered there—employee, contractor, or freelancer hired for a specific task—has been unfailingly patient, clear, and helpful. So thank you Emily Goldman, Nat Razi, and Lynn Brown for saving me from myself, and Viki Lester for the pin. Many thanks to Christine Foltzer for the cover design and, especially, for being patient with my typeface fussiness. To Lauren Hougen, production editor, for organising everything, and Melanie Sanders, who dealt gracefully with a back-and-forth copyedit. To senior associate director of publicity Alex Saarela, marketing director Theresa DeLucci, and digital marketing coordinator Amanda Melfi. Particular thanks to Rovina Cai, who created the gorgeous illustrations for both the cover and the interior.

Outside the Macmillan sphere I want to thank Christina Fanciullo, the librarian who retrieved for me articles defended by paywalls, those twenty-first-century equivalents of moats. To Cheryl Morgan, who pointed me in the right direction for Welsh pronunciation. And to all the friends who heroically did not scowl or roll their eyes when I told them I'd set *Menewood* aside for a few weeks *again*. (And *Menewood* is now finished—so it all worked out in the end.)

Most of all, and always, thanks to Kelley, without whom nothing . . .